"What's got yo[u]... Jake asked

He rested a hand on her shoulder as though that was the most natural thing in the world for him to do.

"You've never had sisters," Maureen replied. "So you wouldn't understand."

"You were talking about trust—I know that. You were wondering how Cathleen could've trusted Dylan so much that she always believed in him—always believed he didn't commit that murder."

"Yes. So?"

"Well, it's got me thinking that's our problem, too. I hurt you and broke your trust. Now I need to earn it back again."

"That's one way to look at it, " she agreed. "Or we could just count our losses and move on."

"But how would that get us any further ahead? Maureen, no matter who you end up with, eventually, at some point, he's going to let you down. The right person, though, will try to make up for it when he's made a mistake."

The right person. Was it really as simple as that? And if it was, how was a woman supposed to know when she'd found him?

Dear Reader,

As I contemplate this last book of my trilogy, I remember how daunted I felt when I began to write it. My first obstacle related to the murders of Jilly Beckett and Rose Strongman, which occurred in A *Second-Chance Proposal*. I'd come to realize that the person I'd thought responsible really wasn't. My readers deserved the truth…but what *was* the truth?

Next, I worried about Maureen, the firstborn of the Shannon sisters. With this character I knew I'd be addressing deeply emotional issues. Her sisters had always seen her as forceful and confident, but Maureen was plagued with insecurities about her failed first marriage and the strained relationship she had with her twelve-year-old daughter, Holly. I wanted Maureen to find peace and happiness in a new relationship with a special man. But the hero I'd selected—Jake Hartman—balked at just the wrong moment. For a while I feared all was lost.

I sat in front of my computer day after day, writing paragraphs, only to delete them an hour later. Less than three weeks remained before the deadline when insight struck. Suddenly, I knew whodunit and why. And that Jake really was the right man, the *lasting* man, for Maureen. From that point on, writing the book became joyful and very satisfying. I hope you'll experience those same emotions as you settle in to visit with the Shannon sisters one last time.

Sincerely,

C.J. *Carmichael*

P.S. I'd love to hear from you! My mailing address is 1754-246 Stewart Green, S.W., Calgary, Alberta T3H 3C8. Please send an e-mail to: cjcarmichael@shaw.ca and by all means visit me at www.cjcarmichael.com.

A Lasting Proposal
C.J. Carmichael

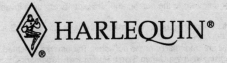

HARLEQUIN®

TORONTO • NEW YORK • LONDON
AMSTERDAM • PARIS • SYDNEY • HAMBURG
STOCKHOLM • ATHENS • TOKYO • MILAN • MADRID
PRAGUE • WARSAW • BUDAPEST • AUCKLAND

ISBN 0-373-71050-X

A LASTING PROPOSAL

Copyright © 2002 by Carla Daum.

This edition published by arrangement with Harlequin Books S.A.

® and TM are trademarks of the publisher. Trademarks indicated with ® are registered in the United States Patent and Trademark Office, the Canadian Trade Marks Office and in other countries.

Visit us at www.eHarlequin.com

Printed in U.S.A.

This trilogy is dedicated to my editors,
Beverley Sotolov and Paula Eykelhof,
with my thanks and affection.

Thanks to those who assisted me in my research, in particular, Corporal Patrick Webb of the RCMP in Calgary, Constable Barry Beales of the RCMP Canmore Detachment and Lynn Martel, a reporter with the *Canmore Leader*.

PROLOGUE

Fall, 1999

IT WAS A NIGHT OF ORANGES, golds and blood, blood red. The sun had not quite set on the Thunder Bar M ranch outside Canmore, Alberta. Yet already clinging to the foothills on the eastern horizon was the harvest moon, heavy and florid. Aspens, dripping in their amber foliage, framed the old log ranch house. At the center of it all raged a bonfire. Prongs of orange flames and spears of thick, black smoke lashed out at the darkening sky.

Two groups, mostly men, stood on opposite sides of the blaze. The oilmen versus the ranchers—a centuries' old animosity.

Max Strongman knew that the men on the other side of the fire saw him as a sellout. He was married to the woman who owned this land. Today he hoped to finalize a deal on her behalf with Beckett Oil and Gas to explore, develop and produce the black gold upon which the wealth of Alberta was based. The CEO of the company, Conrad Beckett, stood beside him with his teenage daughter, Jilly.

There were others. Max's grown son, James. Harvey Tomchuk, Max's retirement-age accountant. Several executives from the oil company, too, as well as lawyers and investment representatives from the nearby city of Calgary.

A deal was imminent, despite Beckett's unexpected posturing as they'd discussed terms a few hours earlier. Max hoped that good food and plenty of expensive wine would nudge the executive in the right direction. Inside the ranch house, his wife and the caterer had huge beef ribs marinating in a smoky-red barbeque sauce, next to salads, breads and more. When the fire died down a little, he would start cooking.

Or so he'd planned. But fifteen minutes ago a gang of men had marched up the lane from the public access road. His wife's son, Dylan McLean, a dark-haired, fiery-tempered man with strong opinions on the heritage of the land his great-grandfather had homesteaded, led the entourage. With Dylan was his cousin, Jake Hartman, a towering blond mountaineer. They were at the forefront of the group of neighboring ranchers and local environmentalists who opposed the deal Max had worked out with Beckett.

This problem Max didn't need right now. The deal just had to go through! He'd staked his future and his son's on this land. Together, they would earn millions—

A movement distracted him. Mick Mizzoni, editor of the *Canmore Leader,* had just stepped forward to whisper something to Staff Sergeant Thad Springer of the local Royal Canadian Mounted Police detachment. Rumors of trouble had drawn both men tonight.

But it was Mick Mizzoni who concerned Max the most. The journalist had been against him from the first day Max had been elected as the mayor of Canmore. Undoubtedly Mizzoni was itching to portray him unfavorably yet again.

Max couldn't let that happen. He had other plans for this land—beyond the oil wells—that required he keep town council and public opinion on his side.

He needed something, anything, to make the protesters appear unsympathetic. Earlier in the day, he'd talked the situation over with the woman he loved, and with his son. They'd agreed that for now all he could do was try to appear more calm and rational than the other side. But was that really his only option?

A fifteen-minute tirade by one conservationist ended. Then an experienced trail guide got up to give *his* spiel. *Would they never shut up?* Max could see Beckett growing increasingly anxious. Conrad had his arm around his daughter, and the girl had started shooting some pointed questions to her dad about his company's environmental standards.

Maybe it was time for Max to have his say. He slipped a hand into his jacket pocket.

A second later, a streak of silver flashed against the carbon sky. Loud pops sounded as a firecracker blazed in a celebratory arc above the crowd, fizzling out just meters above their heads.

After the unexpected explosion came a short second of silence. Then a father's anguished cry filled the void.

"Oh, my God! My daughter's bleeding—she's been shot!"

Crimson blood appeared almost black in the fading light. The liquid seeped over Jilly's chest, overflowing to her father's arms.

There was another second of silence as Conrad Beckett's words, and the image of the wounded girl, penetrated the stunned minds of the surrounding men.

And then—chaos. Someone with first-aid experience rushed forward. Staff Sergeant Springer began barking orders to the crowd. Confused and frightened, everyone was talking, shouting.

Max alone didn't move. Coolly, he analyzed the incident and its most likely aftermath. Jilly Beckett had been shot—but the intended target had surely been her father, Conrad. The cops would figure that the firecracker had been a decoy, covering the report from the gun. But who would be blamed for the shooting?

Someone—dared he hope Dylan—from the group
of ranchers and environmentalists was the obvious
answer. Max held back a smile. His prayers had
been answered. Public opinion would be on his side
now, his and Conrad Beckett's.

"I'm sorry, Mr. Beckett. Your daughter is dead."

Max heard the pronouncement and the crowd's
answering gasp. He remained still as a new possibility suddenly occurred to him. For the first time,
fear squeezed his heart, bringing pain to his chest.
He scanned the crowd anxiously, unable to single
out James in the melee.

Where was his son?

CHAPTER ONE

Two and a half years later

BREAKFAST FOR HOLLY, SHOWER, dress...*don't forget the papers you took out of your briefcase last night...* Maureen Shannon was lost in her mental checklist as she opened the door to snag the morning paper. Clutching the lapels of her old flannel housecoat, she stared at the front-page headline: Oil Tycoon Beckett Commits Suicide.

"Dear God..."

Maureen slipped off the elastic band and unfolded the paper, her fingers suddenly clumsy.

Underneath the headline was a picture of sixteen-year-old Jilly Beckett, the same photo the *Calgary Herald* had used when covering her murder almost two and a half years ago. Next to it was a smaller snapshot, grainy and out of focus. Still, Maureen recognized Jilly's oil-executive father, Conrad, smiling beside his wife, Linda.

Maureen scanned the first paragraph. The facts were blunt. Conrad was dead; he'd killed himself.

Maureen curled her bare toes against the cold of the concrete landing of her Mount Royal home. The Becketts lived in her neighborhood, about six blocks to the north. Their social circles had intersected; she and Linda had worked on a few volunteer committees together.

It was a cool May morning and a westerly breeze tossed Maureen's uncombed hair into her eyes. She flipped it out of the way, then remembered she was dressed in only her thin housecoat.

She withdrew inside, skimming through the rest of the article as she made her way back to the kitchen. Conrad had died in the three-car garage of his showcase-perfect home, sitting in the driver's seat of his idling dark blue Jaguar, while noxious carbon monoxide had pumped into the enclosed space. The suicide was attributed to unrelenting depression over Jilly's death.

Conrad, even more than Linda, had never been the same after it. He'd retired from the board of Beckett Oil and Gas—a company that he had founded and intended to pass down to his only offspring. Then he'd sold all his shares to one of the big American companies—Exxon or Shell, she couldn't remember—

Maureen stopped reading to sniff. That smell… Oh, no, Holly's breakfast! She tossed the paper on the counter and ran to the toaster. Too late. Both slices of bread were edged in black. Knowing her daughter wouldn't eat toast this way, not even if Maureen scraped off the burned part, she threw the pieces out and slipped two fresh slices into the slots.

She eyed the paper, then the clock on the stove. If she didn't leave in fifteen minutes, she'd be late for the office. And she wasn't even dressed. She'd have to finish reading the article later.

Ignoring the sick feeling in her stomach, she jogged up the stairs.

"Holly? Are you finished in there?" At moments like this Maureen would have given up her prestigious address and original oak woodwork in a moment for a second bathroom. Rod had always planned to renovate one day, but he'd never gotten past the looking-at-glossy-brochures stage.

No answer from the bathroom, only the sound of water streaming into the sink. Well, she'd have to skip her shower this morning. Back in her bedroom, she grabbed the first suit and blouse that came to hand, then yanked matching shoes from the shelf above them.

Catching her reflection in the mirror on her dresser, she frowned. The only way to deal with her cowlick was to put up her hair—another five minutes lost there....

Hair fixed, she tore back down the short hall. The bathroom door was still locked, and she could smell—

Damn it to heck!

Maureen raced down the stairs in her low heels and tossed the second batch of ruined toast into the garbage. She checked the clock again. Five minutes.

Back up the stairs.

"Holly, I can't go to work without brushing my teeth and washing my face. And you need to eat. The toaster isn't working so you'll have to have cereal."

The twelve-year-old didn't answer.

Maureen rested her head against the paneled door. From inside, she heard some suspicious sniffing. Holly crying once more. A familiar, helpless pain sapped the energy from her limbs.

"Are you okay?"

The water came on again, blocking out the quiet sobbing.

Maureen knocked. "Please let me in. Holly?"

Still no answer. From past experience, Maureen knew there probably wouldn't be. Holly needed comfort, but she'd never take it from her mother.

Silence descended as the water was turned off. Maureen made quick use of the opportunity to be heard. "Hey, kiddo. You planning to spend the day in there? Want me to rent a video? We could put the TV by the tub. Maybe fill the sink with popcorn."

"It's not funny, *Mother*."

Maureen flinched. When had her daughter perfected that icy, cutting tone?

"I know it's not funny. But I'm going to have to book an extra cleaning with my dentist if you don't let me in soon."

Something slammed. The toilet seat? The medicine cabinet? A second later the door opened, and Maureen lurched forward. Holly stepped back, unwilling even to touch her.

Indeed she'd been crying. Eyes red, cheeks flushed, lips swollen. Maureen longed to hold out her arms, but she knew—oh, how she knew—that her daughter would just back away.

"What is it, sweetie?" A familiar song on the radio, a dream about the old days—either of these, or any of a number of triggers—could have set her off.

"You are *so* insensitive. I can't believe it."

"What?" Maureen stepped to the side so Holly could leave the bathroom. A familiar sense of helplessness had her longing for the simplicity of a two-year-old's temper tantrum.

"It's a year today," Holly burst out. "You didn't even remember. Did you?"

In her mind, Maureen saw the date on the top of the newspaper she'd looked at earlier: May 3. Why hadn't it clicked sooner? She was sure she would have remembered eventually. Maybe when she pulled out her Day-Timer at work or booted up her computer.

"I'm sorry, Holly."

But her daughter had already taken off down the stairs. A second later, the door slammed.

Maureen swallowed an urge to scream, then went to the front window. She caught a glimpse of Holly from the back as she ran across the street toward school. Poor kid—she missed her father so badly.

One year ago today. It was hard to believe.

To Maureen, it felt as though Rod had been dead much longer.

TWO MINUTES AFTER SHE WAS in her BMW, Maureen was on the cell phone, the tiny attached speaker plugged into her right ear. At a red light, she speed-dialed her secretary.

"Looks like I'm going to be a little late for the partners' meeting. Could you pull the files I was working on last week? And order me up a latte, would you, please?"

Next she dialed her youngest sister, Kelly, who lived with her new husband and his young niece and nephew in Canmore, a mountain haven about an hour to the west.

"Sis? Holly threw another crying fit this morning. Should I try a different grief counselor?"

Holly hadn't seemed to benefit from sessions with two previous psychologists and Maureen had given up. But maybe she needed to try therapy one more time…

"It's a year today, isn't it?" Kelly said.

"Yeah." Jeez, even her sister had remembered. What was the matter with her that the date hadn't registered until Holly had pointed it out?

"It's pretty normal for her to be upset. Honestly, sometimes it's you I worry about more. You're so busy being strong for Holly—"

Yeah, right. If Kelly only knew...

"She's just twelve, Kelly. And she's confused. She and Rod were close." From Maureen's point of view, almost too close. But that was just sour grapes, probably. Maureen couldn't pinpoint the moment her doting toddler had begun running to Daddy when she had a problem, instead of Mommy. When Rod died, Maureen had desperately wanted to be there for her daughter. But Holly wasn't interested in a substitute.

"Of course I understand how hard this is for Holly. But you have to consider yourself, as well. You've been working so hard, for so long. Rod had insurance, right?"

"Yes." And lots of it. But only because she'd filled out the application for him, made him sign it, then paid the premiums every year. She'd discovered early in their marriage that she couldn't count on Rod for anything.

A lesson Holly had never learned. No way could she admit that her darling father had died as a result of *his* carelessness. No. In her mind, his death had become her mother's fault. As if Maureen had wanted him to climb that bloody mountain in the first place!

"Well, why don't you take some time off work. You could use the break, and having you around more might help Holly."

"I'll think about it." Maureen hung up the phone, dissatisfied. The answer wasn't for her to spend more time with Holly. The last person Holly wanted to be around these days was her mother.

With the entrance to her underground parking lot in sight, Maureen switched lanes. Now her mood finally lifted. Soon she would be in her office, her sanctuary. Any problem that came up there, she would know how to handle.

THE LOUSY START TO THE DAY had been portentous. At the partners' meeting, Maureen was urged to take on a new child custody case that would have her spending significant time in Edmonton, three hours north of Calgary. She used up her lunch break on the phone with Rod's mom, who called from Winnipeg to commiserate on the sad anniversary.

Maureen listened, feeling for the woman's pain, never letting on that their marriage had been less than perfect, that Rod had been other than the ideal father or that the accident had been anything but bad luck.

Maureen knew better, of course. Because, after

almost fifteen years of marriage, she had known Rod.

Her husband had been addicted to extreme sports. Eighteen months ago, he'd decided he had to tackle Mount Everest. In preparation, he'd signed on with a team to climb Mount Aconcagua, a less-demanding peak in the Andes.

At more than twenty-two thousand feet, Aconcagua was the highest mountain in the world, except for those in the Himalayas. Though the ascent didn't require technical expertise, it would give him an opportunity to see how his body reacted to the drop in oxygen at high elevations.

Unfortunately, altitude sickness had stricken him early on in the climb. Instead of moderating his ascent, Rod had tried to speed up. When his companions noted his growing disorientation, they'd urged him to slow down. But he'd refused until it was too late.

Death, Maureen was told later, can come quickly to those who ignore the early warning signs.

If Rod had gambled with only his life, Maureen could have forgiven him. But his loss had devastated their daughter, and that was hard to absolve.

Especially when Holly's grief seemed to increase its hold with time rather than ease. First she'd lost interest in her friends; a few months later she'd dropped out of the school band. Her latest report card had revealed falling grades, and during parent-teacher interviews Maureen was told that Holly rarely paid attention in class and almost never handed in assignments on time.

With Rod gone, who, what, could help her now?

During dinner that evening, Holly was silent. When Maureen suggested they watch some home videos of her father after dessert, she relented enough to sort through the row of black cases in the bottom drawer of the entertainment unit.

Maureen stretched her feet out on the sofa as her daughter pressed Play. Seeing Rod's face suddenly appear on the TV screen made her entire body tense. Across the room on the love seat, Holly pressed a tissue under her eyes.

Maureen had taken the footage from the back deck a couple of autumns ago as Rod and Holly were horsing around in the abundant piles of raked leaves that Maureen hadn't had time to bag for composting. On the screen father and daughter tumbled and wrestled and shrieked with laughter. But in the tidy family room Maureen and Holly watched in silence.

Maureen was aware of Holly's quiet weeping. She, however, didn't shed a tear. Not until the camera caught Rod smiling at his daughter, reaching out to touch a strand of her almost white hair. The expression on his face was absolutely doting.

The dull pain in Maureen's chest tightened. The video confirmed what she'd always known. Her husband had loved Holly. When he'd been around, he'd treated their daughter like a princess. And that was what Holly remembered about her dad.

Maureen pulled a tissue from the pocket of her jeans and blew her nose. No wonder Holly was so devastated by his death. What man would ever adore her the way her father had?

At ten o'clock Holly went to bed, and Maureen had the house to herself. She put away the videos, stacked a few glasses in the dishwasher, then brewed herself a little coffee, which she mixed with half a cup of hot milk and a teaspoon of sugar.

Memories of Rod and worries about her daughter were too painful to face. Instead she picked up the paper, and in a flash it came back to her. Conrad Beckett's suicide. How could she have forgotten?

Now she read the article again, every word this time. The reporter had been thorough, delving into the event that had led Conrad to the breaking point—his daughter's murder almost three years ago. Maureen had some personal knowledge of the case, since the tragedy had occurred on the ranch of her brother-in-law, Dylan McLean, several years before he'd married her middle sister, Cathleen.

It seemed impossible that in a crowd the size of the one gathered at the ranch that night no one had seen anything. Yet, that was what all the witnesses claimed. The weapon was never recovered. Kelly had been one of the RCMP officers assigned to the homicide. In her opinion, the case would probably never be solved.

That didn't stop everyone in Canmore from having views on the matter. Initially, Dylan McLean had been the number-one suspect. Then later, when James Strongman ran off to Mexico rather than submit to police questioning regarding the subsequent murder of Rose Strongman, James was seen as the most likely villain. But his guilt remained unproved. Also unknown was whether Jilly had been an accidental target. Most people assumed that the shooter had been aiming for her father and missed.

Jilly's death had been such a senseless act of violence. Who could have guessed that the barbecue would get so wildly out of control? What kind of monster brought out a gun at an event where a young girl was present?

Rubbing her eyes, Maureen sighed. Just the prospect of walking up the stairs and preparing for bed exhausted her. Some days it seemed such a struggle to put one foot in front of the other. She could almost understand how Conrad had felt....

Out of habit, she placed her mug inside the dishwasher and then set about getting ready for bed. As she brushed her teeth, she avoided her reflection in the mirror, just as she knew she'd avoided the truth about her daughter for months.

Physically, Maureen still had Holly by her side.

But emotionally, they'd lost contact years ago. And Maureen had no idea how to go about regaining it.

Kelly thought Maureen needed to work less, be home more. They'd discussed this before today's phone call. Given the demands of her law firm, Maureen knew that if she wanted to work less, the only option was to quit.

But then what would she do? Without her six-figure income, they couldn't afford to stay in this neighborhood. They'd have to move—but where?

Only one place made sense. The mountain town where she'd grown up—and left to go to university—where her two sisters and their husbands now lived: Canmore.

She could start her own legal practice there. It would be much smaller and less stressful than her work here in Calgary. Equating to more time spent at home with Holly.

But Holly didn't want to spend time with her *mother*. She'd probably hate the idea of moving. And surely an upheaval, just when she was beginning to adjust to junior high, would be a mistake.

Maureen left the bathroom and collapsed on her bed. God help her, she didn't know what to do. All night, she tossed and turned. Finally, just before dawn, she dropped off. Her last thought was a prayer.

Send me a sign. Tell me the right thing to do for my daughter.

CHAPTER TWO

"YOUR PROFITS HAVE BEEN very healthy, Jake," Harvey Tomchuk said between sips of his coffee. "But given the capital outlays you want to make this year, you could use a cash infusion."

Jake Hartman liked the sound of the phrase. Sort of New Age—like a vitamin or herbal infusion. "Are you talking about a bank loan, Harvey? You know I'm not keen on debt."

"No debt." His accountant helped himself to another cup of coffee from the machine on the counter, next to the Dutch oven that Jake hadn't gotten around to putting away after dinner. "I'm thinking of equity here, as in cash provided to the business by a new investor. Simple enough for you yet?"

"Oh, sure. Now I get it. You want me to find someone with half a mil to invest in my heli-skiing business. That should be a snap."

"You could always ask Patricia."

Jake snorted. He'd rather see his business fold than go into partnership with his mother. Not that he didn't sympathize with her. She'd lost her husband when she was only thirty, and been left to raise on her own a rowdy boy she'd never been able to understand.

That had been tough for her, especially since she'd been determined to shape and mold that boy, who'd happened to be him, in the image of her late, idealized husband. And she'd never let her son forget what a terrible disappointment he'd turned out to be. He'd demonstrated no head for business, hated cities and was awkward and disagreeable at the society functions his mother planned her life around. For all his growing-up years, Jake had resented his mother's efforts to control what he wore, how he spoke, the way he cut his hair.

The only times he felt free and happy were on his summer and Christmas holidays, which he'd spent with his uncle Bud McLean's family, on the Thunder Bar M in Alberta. So it was no surprise he'd moved out here the day he'd finished high school.

His mother was furious and refused to so much as visit him. Out of guilt more than affection, he made an annual pilgrimage east so she could frown at him and heave great sighs of disappointment. Once a week he called to assure her he hadn't killed himself on some godforsaken mountain.

Ask his mother for money? No way.

"I guess I'll think of something," he said. "How much, exactly, should I be looking for?"

Harvey circled the bottom number in a long line of figures. Jake winced.

"Of course," Harvey pointed out, "you could avoid all this by lowering your standards just a tad. No one expects real linen in a remote mountain lodge."

"Not a chance." Jake wouldn't even consider that option. Grizzly Peaks was his baby, his life. Already clients came from all over the world, willing to pay thousands of dollars for the opportunity to ski in the backcountry wilderness of the Rocky Mountains.

But he wanted more. Not necessarily bigger—in fact, definitely not bigger—but the best of everything. One day Grizzly Peaks would be the premier heli-skiing operation in North America.

"Well, I'm sure you'll come up with something. You always do. By the way, planning any mountain climbing this summer?"

"My knees have really been bothering me lately." A reminder that he was closing in on forty. Now he needed the four-month summer break from skiing to rest his old ligaments and joints.

Compounding the problem with his knees was his difficulty in finding a buddy to climb with these days. Slowly but surely his friends had gotten married and started families. A day off for climbing was a luxury they could rarely afford.

"You talk like you're old, Jake. Wait until you're in your seventies like me!"

"At least you picked a good profession. You'll be able to keep running your business as long as your mind remains capable of adding and subtracting."

"Yeah, but the question is, will I want to?" Harvey finished off his coffee. "Well, I guess we're done here. I'll put together the final financial proposal, then you can go out and try to find your money."

Harvey gathered the papers into his briefcase, leaving a copy of the statements on the table for Jake. After a warm handshake, he shuffled out the door. Jake thought he'd left, but moments later the older man poked his head back inside.

"You forgot to take in your newspapers."

There were two in the box. Jake subscribed to the *Calgary Herald* as well as the *Canmore Leader*. After waving off his friend, he took them both to the living room.

The headline in the *Herald* startled the hell out of him. Conrad Beckett had killed himself? God, what a nightmare that whole episode was turning out to be. Jake read the print on page one, then followed the story to page three. Most of it was old history; he knew the case well. In fact, he'd even started a scrapbook.

Now he went to the kitchen to get the scissors and tape, then to his desk, where he pulled out the binder he'd used to collect articles such as this one.

It wasn't morbid fascination that drew him, but a combination of personal interest and family obligations. At one time popular opinion around Canmore had it that his cousin, Dylan McLean, was responsible for Jilly Beckett's death. Now almost everyone thought James Strongman had done it.

James's father, Max, was the current mayor of Canmore. He'd married Dylan's widowed mother, Rose, a long time ago. After Jilly's death, he'd convinced Rose to make out her will entirely to him, cheating Dylan of his father's inheritance. Then, just when Rose had seemed about to change her mind and revisit her will in Dylan's favor, she'd been murdered.

At first Dylan, who was known as a hothead, had been suspected again. Then evidence proving that he'd been set up was found. James, who had no alibi for the night Rose was killed, was the most likely culprit. But he'd escaped to Mexico rather than face police inquiries, and hadn't been seen since.

A convenient and tidy impasse in Canmore's two unsolved homicide cases. Jake, however, wasn't so sure that James *was* the guilty party. Or if so, that he'd acted alone. And others in town shared his doubts.

Carefully, Jake cut out the article and the attached photos. He paused to examine them. First Jilly, then Rose, now Jilly's father. Too many deaths, shrouded in too much uncertainty, for one small mountain town of only ten thousand people.

Jake picked up the local paper next. Ironically, on

the front page of the *Leader* was a shot of Max Strongman and a bold heading: Canmore Mayor Won't Run Again In Fall Election.

Well, that was good news. Jake snapped the paper, then peered again at the picture of Strongman. The man had a distinguished, statesmanlike air, but he was as wily as an old coyote, and manipulative to boot. Jake read about his plans to retire from public office to pursue "other interests." Hah! Jake reached for the phone to call his cousin.

"Did you hear the news about Strongman?" he asked once Cathleen had passed the phone over to her husband.

"Wish I could say it was good news," Dylan said. "But you know, the minute he's no longer mayor of Canmore, he'll be pushing that damn recreational housing project on my father's land."

"Next to the oil wells?"

Dylan's laugh was bitter. "If he goes ahead with this, the development will cut right across the natural wildlife corridor along Thunder Creek."

"We've got to stop him somehow."

"Don't I wish," Dylan agreed. "Our best hope is that we elect an antidevelopment mayor who throws so many roadblocks in Strongman's way he hasn't a chance."

But that wasn't likely. Feelings both for and against development in Canmore ran strong, but lately the tide had definitely been in favor of development. Plus, a new man was in the wings—a shoe-in for the job if Max retired. And he was prodevelopment, too.

"Any other options?" Jake asked.

"Let me see. Why don't we prove Max planned both my mother's and Jilly Beckett's deaths, and that James was merely a pawn in his hands. Once Max is in jail, he'll have a hard time presenting his development plans to town council."

Jake sank into a nearby chair. "Now, why didn't I think of that?" Actually, the two men had discussed the possibility of Max's involvement in Rose's murder to the point of exhaustion. They each suspected that James had tossed that firecracker as a diversion for his *father* to shoot Jilly. Odds on proving that, however, were slim at best.

After a depressing pause, Jake told his cousin about the plans for upgrading Grizzly Peaks.

"So you need a silent partner, do you? Let me think about that. I may know just the person."

"That sounds intriguing."

"Oh, she *is*. But I have to go, buddy. Cathleen's giving me that look...."

"Say no more." Jake hung up, knowing his cousin was referring to the look that every man longed for. The look that meant *Come to bed, darling*.

Lucky guy. Jake hadn't been the recipient of the *look* in a long time. In fact, how long had it been?

Sprawling out on the sofa ten minutes later, with a beer and the remote control, Jake tried to recall the last woman he'd had in his bed. Over the years he'd gone through a series of relationships with a number of women. Each time there'd come a point when demands were made that he'd felt unable to meet. The last one's name had been...Terri-Lynn.

The next one would be...who? The pickings were getting meager, Jake had to admit. Most women around his age were married. He was willing to date younger ones. But even the women in *that* group were mostly paired off now.

Maybe he'd missed his chance. Yet Jake didn't regret ending any one of his failed relationships. So maybe he was born to be a bachelor. It wasn't the worst fate for a man...especially one as busy as he was. Grizzly Peaks took a lot out of him. And now he had to find the equity partner Harvey was talking about.

Jake picked up his copy of the financial papers and scanned the bottom line. Who did Dylan know with that much money available?

MAUREEN WENT TO Conrad Beckett's funeral Tuesday afternoon. She sat near the back of the Riverview United Church, the same church where services had been held for her husband, little more than one year ago. And previous to that, for Jilly Beckett.

Many of the people filling the pews today had

attended those funerals, as well. Certainly Linda Beckett had been at both. Maureen remembered her stopping to speak after Rod's service.

"If you ever need someone to talk to, Maureen," she'd said, squeezing her hand hard, "I'd be glad to help."

Linda's well-meaning kindness had made Maureen feel guilty for not having offered the same to Linda after Jilly's funeral. She'd assumed that family members, and more intimate friends, would be filling that role in Linda's life. And Conrad's. But maybe they hadn't.

The service was over at four. Maureen doubted that Linda Beckett even recognized her when she stepped up to give her condolences. The new widow seemed disoriented. Her sister had guided her through every step of the service as carefully as if Linda had suddenly gone blind.

Maureen left the throng of people with a sense of unease. She'd hoped attending the funeral would provide closure in the whole affair, but she was left feeling even more unsettled.

From the comfortable leather-covered driving seat of her BMW, she was tempted to return to the office but instead went to the Safeway and picked up a rotisserie chicken, rolls and a bagged salad. Usually she had a housekeeper half days, so someone would be home when Holly came from school. But they were between employees right now—the last woman had quit when Holly had tossed her dinner in the garbage without even giving it a taste.

Just as Maureen was pulling into her garage, the cell phone rang. She attached the small speaker into her ear and pressed Talk.

"Hello?" With her free hand, she grabbed the bags of groceries, then entered the house.

"It's me. Cathleen. Dylan asked me to let you know about an opportunity. It's with his cousin, Jake Hartman. Do you remember him from our wedding?"

As it so happened, Maureen *did* remember Jake— a big man with dark blond hair. She'd caught his gaze on her a few times during the ceremony, then later at the reception. At the time she'd been vaguely uncomfortable with the man's open scrutiny.

Now she was curious. "What about Jake?"

"He's looking for new capital for his heli-skiing business. It sounds frivolous, but trust me, it's extremely successful. His profits are amazing."

"So?" Maureen set the grocery bags on the counter. She could hear the muffled, pulsing bass of Holly's music coming from upstairs. Her daughter craved awful stuff these days, heavy metal from bands like Faith Warning and Bitter End. Maureen had asked Holly not to buy those kinds of CDs, so instead she borrowed pirated copies from kids at school.

"I thought you might be interested. You have that

money from Rod's life insurance, and I know how pitiful interest rates are these days.''

Maureen pulled out a bowl for the salad, then a knife to carve the chicken. ''You think I should invest Holly's inheritance from her father in a *heli-skiing business? Cathleen, that's nuts!*''

''Why? Jake's a great guy and Grizzly Peaks has a world-class reputation. With your cut of the profits, you probably wouldn't have to work anymore, unless you wanted to.''

Maureen wondered if this could be it—the opportunity she'd been waiting for. ''Well, I have to admit, I've been thinking of quitting my job.'' The new case requiring all that travel to Edmonton had done it. Or maybe it was Conrad Beckett's funeral. Or the lyrics she'd listened to on Holly's ghetto blaster last week when her daughter was out of the house.

''Then you should definitely check out Jake's proposal. If it appeals, you could move back to Canmore. You'll make a ton of money selling your house, too.''

''How much capital is Hartman looking for?'' It couldn't hurt to check this out. Although the idea of being partners with Jake was a little…disturbing.

Hard to say why exactly. Just that something about the man had set her nerves on edge. The way he kept watching her…

Yet for every time his gaze had been on *her,* her

gaze had been on *him*. Even during the service, when she should have been concentrating on Cathleen and Dylan. She remembered thinking, *that man knows.*

He knows I'm only pretending to mourn for my husband.

CHAPTER THREE

JAKE WAS PLEASED THAT HE'D managed to snag an outdoor table in front of the Bagel Bites Café. From the tray in his hand, he unloaded two coffees in foam cups and two toasted bagels with cream cheese. Out of the back pocket of his jeans he pulled a one-page partnership agreement.

He smoothed the folds from the paper, then placed it on the table in front of the unoccupied chair.

Maureen Shannon was ten minutes late.

No big deal. She was driving from Calgary, so it had to be difficult to time her arrival exactly. He had coffee, a comfortable place to sit and warm sunshine on his face. Settling in his chair, he stretched out his legs and told himself he didn't mind waiting.

"Something wrong, Jake?" One of the women who worked behind the counter was clearing tables. "You seem a little edgy. Mind moving your foot so I can get by?"

Jake shifted his legs and frowned. He wasn't *edgy*. It was just that these damn plastic chairs were too small for someone his size. And his new hiking boots weren't as comfortable as his old ones. And he hadn't put enough cream in his coffee....

Okay, so he was nervous. Embarrassing to admit, but true. He tapped his foot and checked his watch again. Fifteen minutes late.

He didn't know why he was uptight about this meeting. If this didn't work out, he'd find another investor.

Yeah, right. They'd be lining up at his door, checkbooks in hand.

Jake sipped his coffee while he scanned the people passing by. Monday mornings in May were pretty quiet in Canmore. Few tourists this early in the season. And the regulars had their jobs—many of them commuted to Calgary.

He wondered what Maureen's plans were. According to Cathleen, she was toying with the idea of moving. Somehow he couldn't picture her living here, though. Unlike her two sisters, she was obviously a city woman.

Of course, he'd only met her a few times, the last occasion being Cathleen and Dylan's wedding. Her husband had been dead just a few months, so he'd expected her to be pretty shaken up. But she was so together it was almost scary. She'd reminded him of the plastic Christmas trees he saw every season in department store windows. Everything about her was so perfect she didn't seem real—from her appearance, which was all big-city polish, to her take-charge manner, to her perfect composure throughout the ceremony.

She'd been one of the few not to tear up during the exchange of wedding vows. Jake had recognized the cynicism he'd glimpsed within those china-doll blue eyes—he, too, held little faith in happily ever after. But he'd never been married, and Maureen had. What life experiences had put that chilly smile on her soft, pretty lips?

And what was going on between her and her daughter? The only time Maureen displayed any vulnerability was when she was watching Holly. But Holly studiously avoided her mother's gaze at all times. Something was definitely wrong there.

Out on the street a black BMW slowed. The driver skillfully maneuvered the vehicle into one of the parallel-parking spots half a block down from the café. The car shouted "big city," so he wasn't surprised when Maureen Shannon stepped out from behind the steering wheel. Holding her blond hair back with one hand, she checked for traffic before hauling a big leather briefcase from the back seat.

Early thirties, he figured, knowing she was the eldest of the Shannon sisters. She had the composure of a mature woman, and the stride of someone with no time to lose. He watched her approach, appreciating her tall, long-limbed form. She wore a black pants suit with a white blouse. Sunglasses hid her eyes. He removed his own, preparing to flag her down.

She seemed to be talking to herself. As she neared, he saw she was speaking into a small microphone attached to the phone in her other hand.

"Didn't you get my e-mail?"

He could hear her now.

"Don't worry. After this meeting I'll go to my sister's and connect my laptop. You'll have another copy before lunch."

Then she was at his table and smiling brilliantly. "Jake Hartman?"

He stood to take her hand.

"Good to see you, Maureen. How was the drive from Calgary?"

"Beautiful. Absolutely stunning." She removed her glasses to look at him, but the sun was so bright she crinkled her eyes and put them back on. "Great weather, isn't it?"

He agreed, pulling out her chair.

Maureen glanced at the table and frowned. "You ordered for me?"

He shrugged. "To save time. How's your daughter doing—Holly, right?"

Maureen shifted her gaze uncertainly. "She still misses her dad."

"I guess that's to be expected."

Settling her briefcase at her side, Maureen sat.

"Cathleen tells me you have a business proposition."

So there was to be no more time wasted on chit-chat, Jake surmised. It wasn't *his* style; he preferred to ease into serious subjects the way you waded slowly into a cold lake.

No, the deep plunge wasn't his way. But he could be flexible. "I have plans for upgrading my heli-skiing business—Grizzly Peaks. Problem is, I've never liked dealing with banks, so my accountant suggested I look for an equity investor—" what had Dylan called it? "—a silent partner."

"Right. Tell me a bit about yourself, Jake. When did you start this business? What do you see as your strengths and weaknesses?"

She was making him feel like a job applicant. It was amusing in a way. He'd earned enough of a name for himself at Grizzly Peaks that most people around here were well aware of his reputation. But Maureen wasn't from Canmore, and she had every right to know about the man she was considering investing her money with.

"I started Grizzly Peaks about ten years ago on seventy-five hundred square kilometers of un-touched backcountry. Our customers fly in by char-ter helicopter to home base. And they're treated to the best. Besides a hundred thousand feet of vertical skiing, we provide guides, gourmet food and lodging. We've even got hot tubs and saunas and a complete health club in our main lodge."

"Rod always wanted to try heli-skiing," she muttered, tearing off a small corner of her bagel and eating it tentatively, as if she expected it to be laced with cayenne pepper or something.

"It's a total blast. I'll take you and your kid on a complimentary junket one day."

"Oh, I don't think so."

"It's not dangerous if you're with an experienced outfit."

"I've heard that line once too often in my life." She picked up the partnership agreement he'd written and read it through.

Jake leaned back and sipped more coffee. Basically the agreement stated that in exchange for her money, he'd provide annual financial statements and a cut of the profits equal to her stake in the business. He hadn't seen any need to make the agreement more complicated than that.

Watching her read, he felt a new tension, unrelated to the business prospects of this meeting. Damn, but she was gorgeous. Without her daughter around, though, there was no hint of the vulnerability he'd thought he'd glimpsed at the wedding. This woman was tough, he conceded. Yet something about her tight smile and the defiant angle of her chin made him want to touch her hand reassuringly.

He had little doubt she'd slap him if he dared.

"Well?" he asked when she appeared to be done.

She dropped the page on the table with no comment. "You said your accountant prepared some financial projections?"

"Oh, yeah." He'd almost forgotten about them. Now he reached into his back pants pocket and pulled out the folded square package. Seeing Maureen's mouth droop at the sight, he regretted not heeding Harvey's advice and having the report printed and bound professionally. With care he pressed out the stapled sheets, then passed them over.

"Thanks." Maureen checked everything very carefully. As she read, she tore away at the bagel, eating it molecule by molecule. She was only a quarter of the way through the bread when she was done with the documents.

"What about years with poor snowfall?" she asked.

"Hasn't happened yet. Before choosing my location, I researched the weather patterns. We get the best precipitation in the Rockies."

"I see." Maureen didn't look at all impressed. "Also, when you mention sharing profits, I assume that would be before depreciation and amortization?"

He realized she was trying to bamboozle him. Just because his presentation was a trifle unsophisticated didn't make him a fool. "No," he said firmly. "I can't pay out profits without making provision for replacing my equipment as it wears out.''

She gave a slight smile. "Fair enough.''

"So..." He waited as she took another nibble from her bagel. "What do you think?''

Her head dipped in a cautious nod. "Your numbers are fantastic. And Cathleen and Dylan have every confidence you can continue to deliver in the future.''

"So will you before this season is out.''

She slid the sunglasses down her nose a fraction of an inch and peered over the top of the frames. "You seem pretty sure of yourself.''

"Really? I was thinking you could give me a few lessons.''

Maureen laughed and it transformed her entire face. The tension he'd felt earlier tightened like a belt across his chest. He thought again about how long he'd been without a woman....

Then told himself he was a raving lunatic even to entertain the thought. This lady was the antithesis of what he looked for. He preferred women who dressed for fun, not business. Women who could let their hair down, who took nothing seriously, especially not him.

This woman had *baggage*. She was a widow with a troubled daughter. Most scary of all, she brought out feelings in him he couldn't understand, let alone name.

And she had the power to write him a check for several hundred thousand dollars. He couldn't forget that.

MAUREEN WAS SO ENGROSSED in her conversation with Jake that at first she didn't notice the man by the window staring at her. When she gave a casual glance to the side and their gazes connected, she felt a fissure of distaste, and a sense of having seen him somewhere before.

He was tall, in his late fifties, and looked like a golfer, with his overly tanned skin, cotton pants and short-sleeved T-shirt with a collar. Caught staring, he wasn't at all abashed. Just nodded and grinned. Smug. Arrogant. She turned her back and waited a moment before asking.

"Who's that man? Sitting by himself at the window…"

"That's our mayor," Jake said. "Max Strongman. Surely Dylan and Cathleen have told you about him."

"Oh!" She took a second look and was relieved that he wasn't watching her anymore. "Yes, of course. I think we met once, many years ago." She lowered her voice. "Dylan believes Max put James up to killing Rose."

"So do I," Jake said frankly. "James came out for a week of heli-skiing two winters ago. While no coward, I wouldn't call him a deep thinker. He's the kind of man easily influenced by those around him.''

"Do you feel he was behind Jilly Beckett's murder, too?''

"That's trickier, although I wouldn't put that past him, either. Both he and his father seem to have a vendetta against Dylan.''

"Which makes sense,'' Maureen pointed out, "when you consider Dylan has always been their only real obstacle to the McLean property.''

"And all the money from the oil wells and future property development,'' Jake agreed. "No doubt they'd love to see him behind bars. I think Jilly's death was supposed to be a setup for Dylan. At any rate, it stopped the protest that might have delayed their oil deal.''

Maureen tried another taste of the bagel. It was good, but she didn't care for the cream cheese slathered on top. Mention of Jilly reminded her of Linda, who was rarely out of her thoughts these days. One day soon she had to call her....

"I was at Jilly's father's funeral last week.'' She had no idea what had prompted her to tell Jake. But he leaned forward with apparent interest.

"Yeah, I read about Beckett. Very sad.''

"I have this strange feeling that we haven't yet uncovered the truth about the night Jilly was killed, and there may be more lives lost because of it.'' Maureen paused, wondering whether Jake had any clue what she meant, or if he was nodding to be polite.

"I feel the same way. When I see Max Strongman walking the streets of this town, living off the gravy from his dead wife's oil wells, well, I tell you, it just doesn't sit right."

"Even before you told me his name, I had this antipathy toward him."

"That proves you have good instincts."

Maureen knew she did, and for that reason she almost always went with her gut feeling when it was strong. As it was about Jake Hartman.

That was why, despite the potential problems with this heli-skiing business, she'd decided to go ahead with the deal. It would take most of Rod's insurance proceeds, but if the returns were as good as expected, the risk would be well worth it.

Her only hesitation came from the prospect of working with Jake. It concerned her that as a supposedly mature man he was still devoting his life to the toys and games that belonged to youth.

Just like Rod.

Ah, but she wasn't marrying Jake, was she. Merely going into partnership with him. It didn't matter that he was so damn attractive. Or that he seemed to have an uncanny ability to read her mind.

"Cathleen tells me you're considering moving to Canmore?"

"Considering," she emphasized. "*If* I can sell my

place in Calgary, work out a deal with my partners at the law firm, find the right place to buy here in Canmore.'' She smiled ruefully at all the uncertainties yet to be faced.

"Do you have a real estate agent looking for you?"

"Yes. My sisters have hooked me up with Beth Gibson. She used to run a catering business, but I understand she's been in real estate for several years now and is one of the top selling agents in town."

"As well as being an alderwoman on town council," Jake said. "She's quite an amazing person, all right."

Maureen's cell phone on the table rang. With an apologetic shrug, she turned it off after checking the display to see who had called.

"I guess we'd better get our papers signed," he said. "If you don't have any more questions."

Maureen picked up his one-pager, which she'd already scanned, then handed it to him. "I hope you don't mind, but I took the liberty of bringing my own agreement."

He seemed apprehensive as she unsnapped her briefcase, and his eyes definitely widened as she pulled out the twenty-five-page document she'd drafted at home on her laptop last night.

"Why don't you have your lawyer check through this before you sign," she suggested. "Initial any changes you'd like to make, and I'll consider them."

Jake took a few seconds to absorb all this. "And the money?"

"As soon as I receive the signed contract, I'll transfer the funds directly to your bank." She stood, whisking up her briefcase and the phone. "Nice to meet you, Jake."

"You haven't touched your coffee."

"I don't drink regular coffee. For future reference, I prefer lattes. Double espresso and skim milk."

After a brief pause, Jake responded mildly, "I'll make note of that."

Had he thought her rude? "It's just that I can't take coffee without milk anymore."

"Stomach problems?"

She didn't answer, annoyed once more that she'd let their conversation turn too personal.

"Or maybe just too much tension in your life? You know, moving to Canmore would definitely help you with that."

Somehow Jake's eyes seemed to be saying more than his words. As if he *wanted* her to make the move, for his own personal reasons. For a moment she felt a buzz of uncertainty.

This was what she'd been worried about. This undercurrent between them...almost as if...

But no. It couldn't be. It *wouldn't* be.

"Goodbye, Jake," she said firmly. It was past time for this meeting to end.

CHAPTER FOUR

MOVING INTO CATHLEEN AND Dylan's B and B even temporarily seemed a terrible imposition. Unfortunately, Maureen didn't have much choice. Since that first meeting with Jake two weeks ago, fate had pushed her to Canmore. Maureen felt like a reluctant swimmer asked to jump off the diving board at the deep end of the pool.

Seconds after parking her BMW next to her sister's Jeep, Maureen was lugging the top suitcase from the trunk, while Holly ran inside the B and B to announce their arrival. Maureen took the opportunity to grab a few breaths of fresh air. Any second now, chaos would erupt again....

The madness had begun with a phone call she'd placed shortly after signing the agreement with Jake, to a real estate company in Calgary about listing her home. It just so happened that the agent had a buyer willing to pay top dollar for immediate possession. Given twenty-four hours to think about it, Maureen had talked to Holly and her teachers.

Holly claimed not to care what Maureen did. The

teachers considered a change might be in her daughter's best interest.

That had left dealing with her partners about leaving the firm. Here again she'd met with less resistance than she'd expected. They'd been very open-minded about a year's leave of absence. Of course, she would have to finish up a few cases personally. But by and large, the other partners were willing to take on her clients, including that new case in Edmonton.

Now she was more unfettered than she'd been since Holly was born—and scared to death about it. What was she going to do with her time? Certainly not spend it all with her daughter, as Kelly had suggested. On the drive up, Holly had barely spoken. Their relationship was getting worse with every passing day, it seemed.

At the sound of the screen door opening, Maureen braced herself.

"You made it!" Cathleen burst through the door and came barreling toward her. She was wearing jeans, a white shirt and brown boots, her dark hair a tumble of waves framing her wonderfully expressive face. "Oh, Maureen, this is going to be such fun!"

"I'm not sure *Canmore* is big enough for the two of us, let alone this house of yours." Maureen gave her sister a tight hug and a peck on the cheek. "But we do appreciate your hospitality, that's for sure."

"Don't be silly. The lodge is huge. We have lots of room. Here's Dylan. He was working on the books, so don't mind if he's grumpy."

"*You're* the one who gets crotchety doing the books, darlin'. Not me." Dylan stepped off the porch, toward the car. "Hey, Maureen. Let me get those for you." He took a suitcase in each hand, then glanced back at his wife. "Which rooms?"

"Teddy Bear for Holly," she said. "Which would you like, Maureen?"

"The Three Sisters room. If it's free." Located at the front of the second story, the suite had a big bay window with a view of the triple-peaked mountain that the Shannon girls liked to pretend had been named for them.

"All the rooms are empty this week," Cathleen said. "It's still a little early in the season."

"Well, hopefully we'll be out of here before summer," Maureen said. She felt bad about taking up two rooms as it was, especially as both Cathleen and Dylan had refused to accept payment for this stay.

"I'm not trying to get rid of you, understand, but the cutest town house just went on the market. Beth Gibson phoned this morning, and Kelly and I want to show you later. Come inside and let's have a coffee. Poppy's been baking."

Poppy was always baking. Poppy was their grandmother on the paternal side of the family, but none of them had known about her until she'd arrived on

Cathleen's doorstep last summer. The redheaded seventy-year-old had claimed she was a cookbook author who needed a place to stay and work on her latest project.

Not once had any of the Shannon girls suspected that this woman was in fact the mother of their vagabond father, who'd deserted their family shortly after Kelly's birth.

Once Poppy had admitted her true relationship to them, she'd provided the girls with the missing pieces of the puzzle. Apparently, after leaving his family, their father had returned home to the Maritimes and never mentioned his wife and three daughters. Only after his death in a car accident had Poppy discovered the truth.

She'd found it easy to track her three granddaughters to Alberta, but hadn't risked contacting them directly, worried that negative feelings for their father might make them unreceptive to other members from that side of the family. So she'd booked into Cathleen's bed-and-breakfast as a guest, to see how things went from there.

Frankly, Maureen wasn't all that impressed with the subterfuge. But her sisters had taken to their new grandmother unreservedly, to the extent that the elder woman was now an integral part of their lives. Poppy had been managing the kitchen at the B and B since the first day she moved in. And now she baby-sat Billy and Amanda on the afternoons that Kelly had to work and Mick was at the paper.

Poppy was pulling butter tarts from the oven just as Maureen stepped into the kitchen. Holly was at the large oak table, a glass of milk already in front of her. Poppy glanced up from the hot tray with a welcoming smile.

"It's so good to see you, Maureen. My, but you're thin."

"And it looks like you have just the remedy." Maureen accepted Poppy's kiss without reciprocating. Scents of vanilla and toasted pecans emanated from the small baked pastries. "Cath, how do you keep your figure with this woman's cooking to tempt you all the time?"

"Oh, we believe in lots of vigorous physical activity around here." Dylan came up from behind with the suitcases. He winked at Cathleen, whose suddenly pink cheeks told the whole story.

Maureen laughed, then helped herself to a mug. She poured it half full of coffee, topped it with milk, then stuck it in the microwave for forty seconds.

"Can I ride Cascade every day now that we live here?" Holly asked her aunt.

"You bet, kiddo. She'll love the extra attention."

Maureen noticed a beautiful white cat peeking out from under Cathleen's chair. She bent to the floor.

"Hey, pretty kitty. Who are you?"

"Oh, Crystal was Dylan's mother's cat," Cathleen explained. "He found her out on the street the day of his mother's funeral."

"Max kicked her out? Oh, you poor baby."

Coaxed from her hiding place, Crystal allowed Maureen to scratch her under the chin before scurrying from the room.

Three beeps from the microwave announced that Maureen's coffee with milk was hot. She cupped the mug in her hands, then stood to one side as Holly chatted happily with Poppy and Cathleen. It was great to see her daughter so animated. So she *could* be happy. When the right people were around.

Unlike many girls her age, Holly still didn't care much about fashion or her looks. She wore her blond hair short, hadn't asked to pierce her ears and still chose clothing with comfort in mind. Today she was wearing jeans and a T-shirt, and thick gray socks.

Maureen supposed she was a bit of a tomboy, as Kelly had been at that age. Which Rod had definitely encouraged Holly to be.

Another sip of coffee went down like sulfuric acid. The pit of her stomach felt like a witch's cauldron today. Must be the anxiety of the move... wondering whether or not she'd made the right decision. Maureen tossed the remaining contents of the mug down the drain and poured herself water, instead.

"I've put out plates and forks because the tarts are still so warm," Poppy said, serving Holly first.

Maureen noticed that Holly didn't slide away when Poppy put a hand round her shoulders. "You'll be starting at the Laurence Grassi Middle School, will you?"

Holly nodded. "I guess."

Dylan had come downstairs from depositing their luggage. Maureen noticed him trying to catch her eye, his expression unusually serious.

"What's up, Dylan?"

"I was wondering if you went to Conrad Beckett's funeral," he said. "Cathleen and I debated whether or not to attend. In the final analysis we decided against it."

She understood his dilemma. He wouldn't want to stir up old memories of Jilly's murder. "I did go. Linda looked pretty rough."

Guilt nudged as she recalled her good intentions of phoning before the move. But she hadn't had five minutes to spare in the past two weeks.

"Do you think we'll ever know who killed Jilly?" Holly asked.

"Knowing and proving are two different things, kiddo." Dylan ruffled the curls on Holly's head, then straddled the chair next to hers. Again, Maureen noted how her daughter didn't seem to mind being touched, this time by her uncle.

How long would it take, she wondered, until everyone living in this house realized how much her own daughter despised and avoided her? Then one of her little secrets would be out....

That competent, capable Maureen was a lousy mother.

HOLLY *LOVED* HER NEW BEDROOM. It was a little young for a twelve-year-old, but she didn't care. Each teddy bear in the room had its own personality. She'd named many of them on previous stays. Now she took Stanley off one of the shelves and propped him on the bed next to her.

"Hey there, Stanley. Want to know something? You and I are going to figure out who murdered Jilly Beckett." All great detectives had a sidekick, right? Sherlock had Watson. Poirot had Hastings. She would have Stanley.

The bear stared back at her. She imagined him nodding his approval. *Yes. I think I can work with you.*

She pulled her backpack up from the floor and dug out the detecting kit her parents had bought for her eighth birthday. She'd told them she was going to be a detective when she grew up. They—especially her mother—thought it was just a phase, but it wasn't. She was serious, and Jilly's murder was the perfect opportunity to prove it.

The detecting kit was actually pretty cool, even though it was meant for little kids. It had a tape recorder that really worked, a flashlight and a cam-

era small enough to fit in her palm. She checked all
the batteries to make sure they hadn't gone dead,
then returned them to her pack.

She tossed the magnifying glass—it had nothing
on a decent microscope—and opened the spiral-
bound notebook to the first page. To begin, she jotted down the date—she'd seen her aunt Kelly do the
same in the book she kept on her job. Then she
started listing all the facts she knew about the night
Jilly had been murdered.

Soon she had pages of information. When her
mind was finally as empty as the drawers in the
bureau where she'd been asked to unpack her
clothes, she gave up.

"We have a lot of research to do, Stanley."

She tucked the bear under her chin and rolled over
onto her back. The ceiling was white. Just like at
home. If she tried real hard, she could almost pretend...

No. The ceiling was the same, but the smells here
were different. For starters, no one ever baked at her
house. And the sounds—rather, the lack of them—
were strange, too. No cars, or sirens, or rumbling
old buses.

Close your eyes and pretend.

It was her favorite game. Pretend Daddy was still
alive. That he'd been away on a long vacation and
now he was back. He'd pull open her bedroom door
and say, "How's my little angel?" He always called

her that, as if she was something wonderful, almost magical....

How's my little angel? Kind of babyish for a twelve-year-old, maybe. But she hadn't minded. Now no one would ever say those words to her again.

Holly could feel the sadness flowing. It always started this way. The aching would pour into all the empty spaces in her like water, until she was certain she would drown.

But she never did. All she did was cry. Sob and sob, until her head ached and she was tired enough to sleep.

She held up her bear so she could see his eyes. "Maybe you can cry with me sometimes, Stanley. You have a cute little face, but it's sad, too." She hugged him to her.

Daddy, Daddy, Daddy. Come back, Daddy.

MONDAY MORNING, AFTER Maureen had dropped Holly off at her new school, she went with Cathleen to see the town house for sale. The complex was in a cul de sac, backing onto Policeman's Creek, a small branch of the Bow River.

"It's nice here," Maureen commented, turning in a full circle. Tall pines screened the development from the rest of town, and the sound of rushing water was audible from the street. The morning was sunny, and while the air was still cool, the day held the promise of the summer to come. The town homes were stained cedar, with generous windows, and each had its own driveway and attached garage, a welcome luxury in the long, cold winters.

Cathleen stood in front of the unit with the For Sale sign pounded into the small, square lawn. "Beth Gibson said she could get us inside later this afternoon. I suggested just after three-thirty so that Holly could come, too."

"Perfect." Maureen shoved her hands into the pockets of her fleece jacket. She'd slept better than she had in months in the down-duvet-covered bed at the B and B, and her sister and Dylan had done nothing but make her feel welcome. Still, she was used to her independence and longed to get set up in her own home as soon as possible. Plus, she wanted to free up the bedrooms of the B and B for the hordes of summer guests who would soon flock to the mountain town.

Three doors down, someone came out the front door. Maureen and Cathleen turned together, in time to catch Jake Hartman's startled expression.

"Well, hello. Did you come to see me? If so, you went to the wrong number." He had on a thick wool sweater and carried a leather portfolio in one hand. After locking his door, he strolled toward them.

"We were checking out this place that's for sale," Cathleen said. She flashed innocent round eyes to her sister. "Didn't I mention that Jake lives in this complex, too?"

"What a coincidence. No, I don't believe you did." Maureen placed a hand on her sister's shoulder and dug her nails in, even as she smiled at her new business partner. "I would've pictured you in an isolated rustic cabin up in the mountains."

"You've just given a perfect description of the lodge at Grizzly Peaks. Because I sometimes spend weeks away from home, I need a place that doesn't require much in the way of upkeep."

Of course. She'd forgotten she was dealing with someone who played for a living. At least he deserved credit for recognizing his limitations. When she'd become pregnant, Rod had been eager for them to buy a house. But when it came time to mow the lawn or paint the fence, he'd never been around.

"I was just on my way to get new brochures printed," Jake explained. "But if you'd like a quick tour of my place, I believe its floor plan mirrors the town house you're interested in."

"How nice of you to offer." Cathleen sidestepped away from Maureen's grip.

"Brochures?" Maureen asked. "Could I look them over?"

Jake's pleasant expression stiffened slightly. "Sure. If you'd like."

"Definitely. I have a good eye for graphics. I

helped Cathleen with the promotional materials for her B and B. Didn't I, sis?''

''I'll show you the brochures after we go through the house,'' Jake said. He led the two women up the walk and unlocked the front door.

Maureen wasn't so sure she was still interested in the property for sale, now that she knew Jake would be her neighbor. Sneaky Cathleen, not mentioning a word… But there was no way to turn down his offer without sounding churlish.

All three of them removed their shoes in the foyer. Maureen noted the generous front closet, then followed Jake to the main sitting area. Of course there would have to be a gorgeous slate fireplace.

''Is this an upgrade?'' she asked, running a hand down the rough, gray-speckled stones.

''No. All the units have them.''

Damn.

''Come see the kitchen.''

The cabinets were light maple, the countertops large blue tiles. Maureen traced the white grout with her index finger. ''I guess this must be hard to keep clean.''

''Not really.'' Jake smiled. ''A little soapy water and a dishcloth do the trick. Want to have a look at the bedrooms?''

Just as Maureen had her foot on the first tread, she heard her sister say, ''You two go ahead. I need to make a phone call, if that's okay, Jake?''

"No problem," Jake called back, already halfway up the stairs.

Gritting her teeth at her sister's latest—obvious—maneuver, Maureen followed him. All the way she admonished herself not to notice the snug fit of his jeans, the narrow line of his hips and legs, the tiny red label that identified the make of his pants, the way the denim was fading at the stitching points of both pockets....

Good job not noticing, she congratulated herself at the landing. The hall was small, but the town house had three bedrooms, and the master was extremely generous.

"Sorry it's a bit of a mess." Jake gestured for her to enter his room first.

The king-size bed drew her glance. The comforter had been pulled up in an attempt at neatness, but the lumps and bumps suggested his pillows and sheets were not exactly where they were supposed to be. Maureen had a flash of two naked bodies, dim lights, soft music in the background....

Lord, what was she doing? *Focus on the rest of the room, woman! Look at those clothes strewn on the floor. Doesn't that remind you of Rod? You were always picking up after him....*

"There's a view of the creek," Jake pointed out. "At night you can hear it."

Maureen crossed to the window, unable to believe

how perfect everything was. "The sound of the water must be very soothing...."

"Have trouble sleeping, too, do you?"

She ignored his all-too-accurate deduction and checked out the closet. It was spacious. Then the ensuite. Luxurious. Finally, when they reached the extra bedrooms, she identified a problem. "These rooms are way smaller than Holly's back home. I don't think she'd be very happy."

Jake tapped the dividing wall. "You know, this isn't weight-bearing. Dylan and I could probably tear it down for you and make one big room with two closets. What girl wouldn't love that?"

"Holly's not into clothes," Maureen said, although it was beside the point. Chances were most town houses would have small secondary bedrooms. And Jake was right; combining the two rooms would be easy enough. To suggest he would help was generous of him, although of course she could never let him.

Back downstairs, Maureen found a note from Cathleen on the table. *Figured you guys would have business to talk over, so I've driven to Kelly's for coffee. Meet me there.*

"She's gone." Maureen waved the note in the air, then scrunched it into her pocket.

"Those newlyweds are the worst, aren't they?" Jake grinned, making it clear that he'd recognized Cathleen's attempts at matchmaking.

Maureen groaned and sank into one of the kitchen chairs. "I'm the eldest. I'm supposed to be the bossy one. But ever since Rod's accident, my sisters have treated me like the baby in the family. First they pressured me into returning to Canmore. Now they want you and me to practically move in together."

"Moving in might be a little hasty, but would three doors down be so bad?" Jake settled in the chair opposite hers, folding his hands on the table and leaning in close.

Years and the weather had marked Jake's skin. Yet this made him no less attractive. Although she guessed he was nearly forty, his hair was still unmarred by gray, and his blue eyes were a startling shade, much lighter than her own.

In the curve of his mouth and the directness of his gaze, she saw honesty, humor and just a touch of wariness, as if he hadn't quite made his mind up about her, either. Well, that was good. She'd lent him quite a bit of money. Keeping him on his toes was wise.

"Let's see that brochure."

Jake blinked and sat taller in his chair. "Sure." He opened his leather portfolio, which he'd been carrying around, and out slid the prototype for their main advertising pamphlet. "It's basically the same as my previous one, only updated with the improvements we're making this summer."

Maureen reached for the buff paper, prepared to

be disappointed. She'd expected lots of gloss and color. But this was a very plain product. The front cover bore the title "Grizzly Peaks." Below that was a black-and-white photo of a solitary skier in a mass of virgin snow.

She could see the brochure's appeal; it had a certain understated style. But would it attract attention sitting on a rack of similar brochures, all vying for the eyes of the winter tourists?

"Well?" Jake prompted.

"Two points concern me right now. First, if I hadn't happened by this morning, you would've had these printed without running them by me first. I'm not sure that's a very good start for our partnership."

She suspected she'd annoyed him, but when he replied, his voice was calm. "I hadn't counted on you being involved in the day-to-day decisions."

"Really? I don't remember any limitations on my involvement in our partnership agreement. But back to the brochure... It lacks visual punch, don't you think?"

"Visual punch?"

"I pictured something eye-catching, of obvious quality. An offering that would stand out from the racks of brochures you always see at the information center."

"And *I* think that when you print on recycled paper, you send out a message about the environment. All my booklets, cards and stationery are on this type of paper.''

''Okay, I can concede that point. But I still believe we could do a more effective sales job with our copy. Frankly, we could use a good slogan. Something to pique the readers' interest the moment they pick up the brochure.''

''I suppose…''

''Plus, the information and fee structures in here are all geared to the individual. Have you thought of trying to appeal to families? Or even couples looking for a different, yet romantic, getaway…? Say!'' An idea hit her. A good one. ''We could even offer a wedding service, a full-package deal. I'll bet there are people who'd love to get married on a pristine mountaintop. What do you think?''

''I don't know.'' Jake drummed his fingers on the kitchen table. ''Interesting idea, I suppose, but have you considered the difficulties? Flowers, for instance. Flying flowers up the mountain would be damned expensive.''

''Jake, it almost seems as if you're not interested in my ideas.''

''Well, of course I am.''

He put a hand to his face. Was he covering a smile?

''I just didn't expect you to have so many of them.''

CHAPTER FIVE

"Isn't this great?" Kelly said, bringing a third coffee mug to the table. "Now that you're back, Maureen, we'll be able to get together all the time."

"It *is* great," Maureen agreed. She'd refused Jake's offer of a ride, instead choosing to walk the six blocks from the town house complex to Kelly and Mick's home. She'd found Cathleen and Kelly in the kitchen, sitting at the table by a big bay window, watching Billy and Amanda. The five- and three-year-old were outside kicking around an old soccer ball.

"They're such independent kids," Kelly said. "Very easy to take care of."

Of course they'd learned that independence the hard way. Their mother, an alcoholic, had eventually abandoned them. Recently she'd asked her brother-in-law, Mick, and Kelly to take permanent custody.

"They seem much happier than they did at Christmas," Maureen noted.

"A lot has changed since Christmas," Kelly said. Maureen noticed her fingering her new wedding band. Kelly and Mick had married last December.

It had been an expeditious union, undertaken for the sake of the children, or at least that was how it had started out.

"You're really happy, too, aren't you?" Maureen asked.

Kelly nodded and smiled. "Mick is the most amazing man. And the kids…"

"You should see them when they visit," Cathleen said, watching as Billy held the ball in place so Amanda could give it a good whack. "Amanda is developing into a real tomboy. And Billy is so helpful. He always insists on cleaning out Cascade's stall."

"What about Sharon? Have you heard from her lately?"

Kelly sighed. "That's my biggest concern these days. She hasn't called the children in about three weeks, even though she knows we're happy to pay for the charges. She's living at the ski resort in Whistler, working in one of the bars. The worst lifestyle for someone with her drinking problem. Mick and I worry so much…."

Maureen gave her a hug. "Nothing you can do about it, Kel. Sharon's a grown woman."

"I know. I just think those kids deserve more from their mother. Anyway…enough doom and gloom. Tell us what you thought of the town house."

Maureen leaned back in her chair and fixed Cathleen with one of her best, superior, big-sister glares. "Why don't you two level with me? It's not real estate you want me to buy. It's a man."

"It's been over a year since Rod died," Kelly said tentatively. "We thought it might be time."

"Maybe. But Jake Hartman? Honestly, just because we're both available doesn't make us a winning combination."

"Have you got something against blond, rugged good looks?" Cathleen asked. "Or maybe it's the fact that he's tall, obviously in excellent condition and, did I mention, running a *very successful business.*"

"Oh, he's a hunk, all right," Maureen conceded. "And he may even be well-off. But dig a little deeper and what do you find? A man near forty whose life revolves around fun and games. Definitely not my type."

Kelly looked across the table at Cathleen and shrugged. "Well, what about the town house?"

"That had possibilities," she admitted. More than possibilities—it was practically perfect. But she still had to get her head around also being three doors down from Jake Hartman.

Never in a million years would she admit as much to her sisters, but what really bothered her was that she *did* find the man attractive.

Maureen considered herself an intelligent woman. She didn't like to think she was the type to make the same mistake twice. But perhaps something in her genetic makeup drew her to good-looking yet immature men. How else to explain the erotic thoughts that had struck the minute she'd stepped inside Jake Hartman's bedroom? Thankfully the man was not a mind reader, or she'd be too embarrassed to work with him.

Her sisters, however, were proved mind readers. And the way they were smiling at each other right now confirmed that her hormonal impulses had shown.

The best defense… "I insist that you put a stop to this matchmaking business. Jake and I are business partners, and *only* business partners. Besides…" She had a trump card, and now was the time to play it.

"Holly is still so broken up about Rod's death. I honestly don't think she could cope if I started dating again."

MAUREEN PICKED HER DAUGHTER up after school that afternoon, planning to drive straight to the town house to meet the real estate agent.

"How was the first day?" she asked.

Holly had just flung her backpack into the rear seat. Now she did up her seat belt, bending her head so that her blond curls screened her expression.

"Okay." She leaned forward to change the radio station. Abruptly, the raw edgy music of the Tragically Hip replaced Glenn Gould's performance of Bach's D minor piano concerto. Maureen didn't mind. Nothing on Canadian airwaves could be as bad as what Holly chose to listen to in the privacy of her bedroom.

"Your aunts have found a town house they thought we might like," Maureen explained as she took the route back to the cul de sac she'd visited with Cathleen that morning.

"Already? I thought we were staying at the B and B for a long time."

Her daughter sounded as petulant as a preschooler. Maureen signaled for a right-hand turn and took a deep breath. "Even if we like this place, we can't have possession for six weeks, so we won't be moving right away."

"Six weeks! Why can't we live at the B and B forever? There's lots of room—"

"Believe me, after six weeks it won't seem like so much room anymore." Especially not to Cathleen and Dylan.

Beth Gibson, an attractive woman in her fifties, was waiting in her car when Maureen pulled up to the side of the road.

Maureen put on one of her professional business smiles and met Beth on the sidewalk in front of the For Sale sign.

Holly trailed behind. "This is *it?* It's so *small.*"

Maureen should have known not to expect any

positive comment. Still, to keep her tone upbeat took effort. "Not as big as the house, I know, but just think. Hardly any lawn or gardens to worry about, and only that single driveway to shovel when it snows."

"As town homes go, these are quite spacious," the agent said. "Hi, good to see you again, Maureen. This must be your daughter, Holly."

A wristful of gold bracelets jangled as Maureen shook hands with the woman. By Canmore standards, Beth, in her suede pants and beautiful hand-knit sweater, was almost overdressed. Blond highlights disguised the gray in her carefully styled hair and her makeup was discreet but effective in camouflaging the aging that most women begin to notice in their midforties.

"Nice to meet you, Beth. I'm looking forward to going inside. Cathleen and I were by this morning, checking out the exterior."

"So you've seen the creek? Lovely, isn't it? Wait till you catch the view from the kitchen. Coming, Holly?"

Inside, they all removed their footwear, then Maureen followed Beth, while Holly struck out on her own brisk tour. Maureen was still in the kitchen—a bright, well-laid-out room—when Holly resurfaced.

"I've seen everything. I'll wait outside."

"But did you like—" Maureen stopped talking. Her daughter was gone. She turned to the French doors, which opened to a small balcony with room for a table and chairs and an outdoor barbecue. With the creek up front and mountains in the background, what a setting this would make for early-morning coffee and a leisurely read through the weekend paper....

She was going to put in an offer, Maureen realized, unless Holly had any violent objections. This unit was every bit as nice as Jake's, except that it could use a fresh coat of paint and maybe new carpet in the living room. On the plus side, the basement was finished, so Holly would have a place where she could invite friends and not feel she was tripping over her mother.

Or vice versa.

"Are the window coverings included?" she asked Beth.

As soon as he drove up to the town house complex, Jake recognized Maureen's car. Shining black, it had to have been washed in the past day or two. This time of year, with melting snows and frequent rains, most vehicles were plastered in road grime.

Their encounter that morning had taken a toll. Set back the production of brochures by at least a week and edged his blood pressure up a few points, as well. He didn't know whether to be amused or annoyed. Harvey had suggested a *silent* investment partner, but Maureen was anything but.

Jake hit the button of his electric garage opener and was about to pull into the single parking space when he noticed a young girl leaning against the passenger door of the BMW. Holly, Maureen's daughter.

Instead of disappearing inside the garage, he left his vehicle in the driveway and walked back to say hi.

"Holly? I'm Jake Hartman."

The young girl wore flared jeans and a light-brown leather jacket. Her blond curls might have been combed through that morning, but they didn't look it now. Her eyes, deep blue like her mother's, transmitted mild suspicion tempered with curiosity.

"The one with the heli-skiing business?"

"Exactly." He glanced back at the unit for sale. "Is your mother in there?"

"Yes. Taking *forever*."

Jake smiled. He remembered the days when fifteen minutes could seem that long. "Would you like to see some pictures of Grizzly Peaks? That's the heli-skiing company your mom is investing in."

"That would be cool," Holly conceded. She pushed away from the car door and followed him to his house. Once inside, she glanced around the rooms with halfhearted interest.

"Do you like the town house?" he asked. "Do you want your mother to buy it?"

"I'd rather stay with Cathleen and Dylan," she

said, slipping out of her lace-up hiking boots. "They have a horse and a dog and a cat. My great-grandmother lives there, too."

Jake led her to the kitchen. He dug through the pile of papers by his phone. "Here are some photos we took for publicity purposes. Look at that snow! Isn't that something? Do you ski, Holly?"

"Yeah. My dad taught me." Holly moved aside a few days' worth of newspapers and pointed to his scrapbook. It was open to the article he'd recently added on Conrad Beckett's suicide.

"What's this?"

"Just a case I've been following. I suppose you're too young to remember—"

"The Becketts lived in our neighborhood. Jilly used to be my baby-sitter."

"Is that right?" Jake picked two colas from his fridge and tossed one to Holly. The move surprised her, but she caught the can easily.

"Yeah. I hardly remember her, though. I think I threw up on her once. She didn't baby-sit again for us after that."

"No?" He laughed. "I guess not."

"Most people believe James Strongman killed Jilly, don't they? But no one's been able to prove it."

"That's right." Jake straddled one of the kitchen tables and waited to see where this was headed.

Holly had the kind of face that spoke volumes. He could tell that this mattered to her.

She flipped the pages of the scrapbook back to the beginning. "I wonder if *anyone* will ever figure out what really happened that night."

"I'd like to think that one day we'll know." He'd *like* to, but he didn't really believe it would happen. Not all crimes were solved the way they were on the TV police shows that Holly probably loved. And with each year that passed, the chances of uncovering the truth became that much more remote.

"Could I borrow this scrapbook?" Holly asked.

God, she was a serious, intense little thing. Twelve, he remembered, but she seemed younger because she was so small. "Why?"

She didn't answer. "I'll be real, real careful with it."

Was it some kind of ghoulish fascination with crime? He didn't think so. There was a spark of determination in her eyes that reminded him of her mother and gave him a pinprick of uneasiness. Still, there was nothing in the scrapbook that wasn't easily available at the public library....

"Sure. Go ahead."

"Thanks." She shoved his scrapbook inside her backpack, then said, "I guess I should be going."

She didn't sound as though she wanted to leave. Still, he walked her to the door, then followed her outside to the landing. There was Maureen, in conversation with Beth Gibson on the sidewalk between their two cars. Her wavy blond hair glowed in the late-afternoon light. He admired the way her casual fleece jacket and slacks hung on her lanky body.

Having seen her in both her big-city garb and this more relaxed style of dress, he had to say he preferred the latter. What surprised him was that she carried off each look equally well. A bit of a chameleon, Maureen Shannon. He wondered which would end up suiting her best in the end.

SUNDAY MORNING, VERY EARLY, Maureen was surprised to receive a phone call from Jake.

"I'm making an unplanned trip up to Grizzly Peaks today. Wondered if you and Holly would like to come along. Figured you'd like a firsthand look at your investment."

"This would be in a helicopter?" she asked hesitantly.

Jake laughed. "Unless you're interested in a backpacking excursion."

"Um. No, thanks. The helicopter will be fine." She'd never been in one before. Nor had Holly. She hoped her daughter would think this was a great adventure and not complain too much about having to get out of bed early on a weekend.

She needn't have worried. Holly was thrilled at the prospect, especially since Jake was coming along. Maureen didn't know how it had happened so quickly, but Jake had definitely won her daughter's affection.

Jake picked them up and drove to the landing pad where the helicopter was already waiting. Maureen was glad the weather was clear. She was a little nervous.

Of course Jake discerned her unease. He held her hand tight, forcing her to pause when she went to step into the helicopter.

"It's going to be fine," he hollered, over the *thwack, thwack, thwack* of the rotating blades and growling idle of the engine. "Wally's been flying for years. He's the best."

"I have no doubt." She tugged her hand away and followed her daughter inside. Oddly, it was less noisy inside, and more roomy than she'd expected. She smiled at the pilot, then sat next to her daughter on the long bench seat.

Last in was Jake, and then they were off. The sensation of rising straight up was peculiar, to say the least. Maureen focused on the dizzy, dazzling view. "Look, there's Grassi Mountain. When I was young I used to hike in this area all the time." At first with her mother and sisters, then later with girlfriends, even a boyfriend or two. "Now I can't remember the last time I was out in the mountains."

"Daddy and I used to go hiking a lot," Holly told Jake. "Our first hike every year was to the top of Heart Mountain."

"That's a difficult scramble, especially near the end, with all the loose stone. Good for you, Holly."

Maureen felt Jake looking at her as if to say, *And where were you during all of this?* She wished he *would* ask the question so she could tell him she'd been working to pay for the hiking boots, the rain-proof pants and jackets, the deli-packed lunch Rod always insisted on taking along.

But of course he didn't and she didn't. Instead, she shifted her attention from the window on her right to the view out the left. Thank heavens neither she nor Holly had motion sickness.

"My dad was really good at lots of things," Holly continued. "He taught me how to downhill ski and to ride a horse. I would've started show jumping except *she* wouldn't let me."

"What can I say?" Maureen knew her voice sounded tight and hard. "I'm just one of those mothers who hates to see her daughter have a good time."

The trip was longer than Maureen had expected, and she panicked a bit as the helicopter descended. She didn't know how the pilot did it, landing perfectly on the concrete pad built a hundred meters from Grizzly Peaks Lodge.

Ten minutes later, Maureen acknowledged that she'd bought into a piece of true, pristine wilderness. The panoramic views had her turning circles on herself. The beauty transcended the physical; in fact, it was powerfully spiritual. And so peaceful. Maureen filled her lungs and tried to decide how it made her feel. Ten pounds lighter and ten years younger.

"You've done an incredible job with your buildings," she commented as they followed Holly, who was skipping ahead. "The small chalets, even the main lodge—they just seem to *belong*."

"One day I'd like to be open year-round," Jake confided. "This is a great starting point for hiking, fishing and mountain biking in the summer. Up until now I've focused on the skiing crowd."

Jake had packed a lunch, and after he'd finished giving them the tour, they settled by the creek that passed just behind the back deck of the lodge.

There were baguettes stuffed with meat, cheese and sprouts, beautifully cut veggies with a container of dipping sauce, a thermos of lemonade and a whole array of baked cookies and squares.

"This is fantastic," Maureen said, amazed.

"I'm good at sandwiches," Jake admitted. "But I bought the treats at the bakery."

Holly selected one of the vegetarian baguettes and started strolling along the creek.

Maureen spread out on an old blanket. The sun was directly overhead now, and she removed her jacket to use as a pillow once she lay down. She felt Jake watching her, and when she turned and caught him at it, he smiled.

What was he thinking? With Jake, she could never

tell, and that was a big disadvantage. She felt she'd pegged him pretty accurately as a man whose life revolved around the superficial—having fun, seeking thrills and avoiding commitment along the way.

On those moments when his gaze caught hers, however, she saw hints of sincerity, caring and intelligence that defied her easy categorization of the man. Worse was the feeling that when he looked at her, he saw much more than other people did—even her sisters.

It was this attribute in particular that made her most uncomfortable in his presence. And today it reminded her that he knew so much more about her than she did about him.

"Dylan says you were an only child, Jake. What was that like?"

"Pure hell." Jake was straight-faced for a moment, before he smiled. "Just me and my mother most of the time. But I came out to Uncle Bud's ranch every Christmas and summer holiday. I can't tell you how much I enjoyed those trips. Mostly it was the freedom to run around and be myself."

"You didn't have that at home?"

"My mom liked schedules. I had my chores and my homework. Violin lessons and debating club. Mom didn't approve of any of the sports I was crazy about."

"How awful for you."

"I'm sure it was no picnic for her, either. I was

a big disappointment. But I hope she's over it by now. She remarried a few years ago. I think she's happier than she's ever been.''

Maureen was keeping an eye on Holly as she listened to Jake. Her daughter perched on a flat rock by the water, about twenty meters away, and had taken off her shoes to trail her toes in the cool stream.

''Careful not to fall in,'' Maureen called out.

''Oh, Mother. Chill, why don't you.''

Maureen felt as though she'd been slapped. Hiding her reddening face by leaning over the container of veggies, she rejected the idea of rebuking her daughter. Instead, she grabbed a handful of carrots and celery, not bothering with the dip. She nibbled on the vegetables, then leaned back, her face tilted toward the sky.

The sun was so nonjudgmental. It spread its warmth over everybody, everything. Even though her eyelids were closed, she guessed Jake was watching her again. Probably thinking what a witch of a mother she must be, since her daughter so obviously couldn't stand her.

SHE HAS GREAT BREASTS, Jake thought, observing how the soft blue cotton of Maureen's turtleneck molded against her skin as she baked in the noon sun. An age-old reaction had him shifting his sitting position and the direction of his gaze.

This was supposed to be a business trip, yet his feelings had been totally unprofessional ever since he'd picked Maureen and Holly up early that morning.

Jake had to admit he was confused. Every time he saw this woman, he felt a pull stronger than the last time. He wished he could make sense of it. Once again he acknowledged that with her strong personality, she was the last woman he would've expected to be drawn to. And she'd certainly given him no signs of encouragement. Or discouragement.

Unlike other women, she transmitted few clues to how she felt about him, period. Sometimes he imagined he spied interest and mutual attraction in her gazes. Other times he was certain she was too focused on her daughter, and whatever troubles lay in her past, to even notice he was there.

"Was the move hard for Holly?" he asked finally.

Maureen sighed. "I'm not sure. She *said* she was okay with it and she wasn't all that happy in Calgary. She still...she really misses her father."

"I can tell." He waited to see if Maureen would say anything more. Holly's problems today seemed to have more to do with her mother than her father. He poured two glasses of lemonade and passed one to her.

"Thanks." She took a sip. "We've had a bad year, it's true. But I keep remembering Linda Beckett and what she's endured the past few years. At least Holly is alive. She may hate my guts at times, but she's here and I can see her and talk to her and—"

Maureen's voice broke, and she averted her head. Jake sensed that for Maureen, the worst thing was to let someone know she was in pain. She was always the strong one…and in a way he respected her for it.

But at the same time, he didn't think maintaining a stiff upper lip was going to heal the deep rift between mother and daughter.

Holly was suffering. Clearly she missed her father, and undeniably he'd played an important role in her life. And Cathleen had mentioned that the hours Maureen put in at work had always been onerous. Maybe she'd furthered her career at the expense of her daughter's happiness.

Jake knew better than to judge. Most situations were more complicated than they appeared. But he couldn't help thinking that Maureen had given her daughter so much space she'd become lost in it.

CHAPTER SIX

MONDAY AFTERNOON, JAKE was returning calls on his answering machine when the doorbell rang. He left the appointment book open on the table and went to see who was there.

Irrationally, he'd hoped it might be Maureen. But it was Holly on the landing, her backpack lopsided on her shoulders. He checked his watch. "Just finished school?"

She nodded. "I brought back the scrapbook."

He'd been feeling vaguely uneasy about having lent it to her. So this was good. He stepped aside for her to enter.

Holly dumped her backpack on the floor, then started rifling through it. Out came a new-looking agenda, a nylon-covered binder, a tattered lunch bag. Finally, the scrapbook, not much the worse for wear.

Jake stuck it on the hall table. "Want a soda?"

"Sure." Holly slipped out of her boots. In her stocking feet, she was especially tiny. If she was going to match her mother's height, she still had a lot of growing to do.

Jake led her to the kitchen. Holly settled at one of the chairs and pushed back at her hair with a gesture she would have avoided had she realized it was so like her mom's.

"Find anything interesting in those articles?" he asked as he opened the fridge door.

"Sort of." She held up one hand, ready this time to catch the cola he tossed. After popping the tab and taking a long drink, she pulled a small spiral-bound notebook from her jacket pocket.

Watching her flip through the pages, he struggled to stop from smiling. *Miss Organization.* That had to be another reason for the friction between mother and daughter. They were too damn much alike!

Holly started reading. "The first question is, why was Jilly killed? There are two possibilities. One, she was an accidental target. Whoever shot her planned either to kill someone else or not to kill anyone, just stir things up."

"With you so far." Jake straddled a kitchen chair, impressed, despite his earlier amusement.

"The other possibility is that Jilly *was* the target. In which case, the question has to be *why.* Why would anyone want to kill a sixteen-year-old girl?"

"I've never been able to make sense of it," Jake confessed. "Now, if her father, Conrad, had been shot, that would've been another story. Conrad's death might have changed everything."

Jilly leafed ahead in her notebook. "Jilly *was*

standing right beside her father. So he *could've* been the intended target.''

"That's the most likely scenario, from my point of view. Unfortunately, it doesn't help, does it?"

"I don't agree. If we understand the *why*, I'm sure that would lead us to the *who*."

Jake was pretty sure he'd read that line in a mystery novel once. Maybe she had, too. "Could be you're right," he conceded.

Out the window he noticed the afternoon sun glinting off the creek. The stream made him recall Maureen and the trouble she had sleeping at night. He wondered if she'd put in an offer for the place down the street yet....

He was doing it again. Thinking of her. This preoccupation with the eldest Shannon sister was becoming annoying. Or maybe it was simply inevitable. In which case it was time he did something about it.

Jake got up from the table and went back to the fridge, where he opened the freezer compartment. He ought to start supper. Hopefully, if the food smelled good, Holly would stay. Then he might be able to convince her mother to join them, too.

Spying some ground beef, he considered making spaghetti. That was something most kids liked. He put the package of frozen meat in the microwave to thaw, then gathered an onion, some garlic and half a green pepper, which was only slightly shriveled.

He put the Dutch oven on to heat, then started chopping. Holly, who'd been mulling over her notes with a frown, suddenly snapped her book shut. "I've got to figure out who did this. I've just *got* to."

Why the fierce intensity? Jake set down his knife for a moment and regarded the unusual young girl. "Does it help you forget how much you miss your dad when you're busy focusing on other things?"

Holly's eyes opened wide. God, they were replicas of her mother's. "I'm going to work for the RCMP when I grow up. Like my aunt."

"Yeah? Does your mom know about this?"

Her thin shoulders rose and fell. "She wouldn't care."

"I'm sure she would."

Holly said nothing to that and Jake figured it would be foolish to press the issue. He scraped the chopped veggies into the pan of hot oil and stirred them.

"Can I help? I like to cook. My great-grandma's teaching me how."

"You could keep these from burning while I open a can of tomato sauce." He handed her the wooden spoon.

"What're we making?"

"Spaghetti. Want to stay for dinner?"

"Could I?"

"Sure." He reached back into the cupboard for

spices. Nonchalantly he asked, "What about inviting your mother, too?"

Faster than an avalanche could strike in the backcountry, Holly's expression fell. "Do we *have* to?"

"She must be wondering where you are. Unless you called...?"

"I told her I had some research to do. She probably thought I meant at the library. She was going to pick me up at five."

Jake felt a jolt of dismay. "It's past five now."

Holly just shrugged. "I suppose I could try her cell."

Moving way too slowly for his taste, she returned to the table where he'd left the portable. With calm deliberation she punched in seven numbers, then waited.

"It's me," she declared when the call was answered. A long minute passed while she rolled her eyes in a show of boredom.

"Chill, Mother. I'm at Jake's," she said finally. "You can pick me up here."

He was chopping lettuce for a salad when she sauntered back to the counter. "Should I set the table for three?"

"I guess. She might be too mad to eat, though." Jake got the plates out of the cupboard and passed them to Holly. "Why do you do that to her?"

"What do you mean? I meant to let her know— I just forgot."

"She must've been worried."

Holly's expression suggested he was deranged. "Are you kidding me? She's just put out because I disrupted her schedule."

"Come on, Holly. Do you think that's fair?"

"You'd understand if you'd seen the way things were at our house." Bitterness sharpened her words now. "My father was the only one who loved me, as much as my mother tries to pretend otherwise. It's her fault he died, you know."

The unexpected accusation made him pause. "What do you mean?"

"I heard them arguing the night before he left. He couldn't stand being around her. That's why he was always going on these trips. If she'd just left him alone instead of constantly nagging at him, he'd still be alive...."

Holly was fighting back tears, and Jake wanted to offer her something—comforting words...a hug?— to make her feel better. But she had her back to him, obviously making a huge effort to hide her distress.

He contrived an excuse to leave the room so she could pull herself back together.

Holly's attempts to blame her mother for Rod's weaknesses were only natural, he supposed. Kids had a habit of oversimplifying things. Holly had decided her father was the good guy and her mother the villain. In real life, roles were never that simple. But it might take Holly a while to figure that out.

The sound of the doorbell was a mixed blessing. He was eager to see Maureen, but a little worried about Holly's reaction. He pulled open the door cautiously.

BE CALM, MAUREEN COUNSELED herself. Jake stood in the foyer, smiling but obviously concerned.

"Is she here?"

He nodded, then stepped aside. "Come in. I've made spaghetti. Would you like to join us for dinner?"

Only then did she notice the spicy aroma that pervaded his home. Next she focused on his use of the word *us*.

"Have you already invited Holly?"

"Yeah. If that's okay with you?"

She sighed, then dropped her purse and jacket on the floor next to her daughter's backpack. Jake snagged them and hung them in the closet.

"Holly's in the kitchen."

Maureen marked his cautious expression. He was trying to tell her, without words, not to lose her cool. She knew he was right. Yelling and screaming wouldn't accomplish anything.

Still, at her first glance of her daughter, keeping her words calm was difficult. Holly didn't offer a hello, let alone an apology. That she was making herself useful by setting the table was ironic. She was never this helpful at home.

"Holly, you didn't go to the library at all, did you?"

"I didn't say I was going to the library. I said I had research to do."

"Here at Jake's?"

She nodded.

Rather than press for more answers, Maureen chose to sink into one of the stools at the counter.

"How about a glass of red wine?" Jake said.

"That would be wonderful."

He had a bottle uncorked already. With a flourish, he filled two glasses and handed her one. She sipped at it slowly, frankly surprised at the domestic scene before her. Tomato-and-meat sauce simmered in a Dutch oven; a large pot of boiling water sputtered next to it. On the counter was a bowl of tossed salad and, next to that, a hand-sliced loaf of Italian bread in a pool of crumbs.

"We should call Cathleen and Dylan and let them know we'll be eating out," she said.

"I'll do it." Holly took the portable phone into the living room.

Maureen let the air out of her lungs in a long whoosh. "What's going on here, Jake?"

"I wish I could tell you." He leaned over from the kitchen side of the counter. His smile was reassuring as he raised his glass and clinked it gently against hers.

"To teenagers," he said softly.

"She isn't even thirteen yet." Maureen didn't know how she would cope if this antagonism of her daughter's got much worse. She'd panicked big-time when she hadn't found Holly waiting at the public library. After checking with all the employees, she'd become even more worried when it was clear that Holly had never made an entrance.

Who could have guessed she would end up at Jake's? *Why* had she ended up here?

Jake must have seen the questions in her eyes, because he grabbed a damp cloth and started wiping the already clean counter. Recognizing the evasion, Maureen decided against pushing him for information, but she couldn't stop a flood of bitter resentment.

Now Jake was on the inside with Holly, too. Maureen was the outsider, the only one her daughter didn't trust. Bending over the glass of wine, she pretended to enjoy its bouquet, while she blinked rapidly.

"This is nice," she said. Truthfully, she'd barely tasted the wine. Its warmth as it hit the pit of her stomach, however, was something she appreciated.

"Did you put an offer in on that town house?" Jake asked.

"Yes. Beth wrote it up last night. Two hours ago she called with the news that the owners accepted." She lifted her chin and smiled, pushing her negative thoughts to the back of her mind. "Looks like we're going to be neighbors, Jake."

THE ATMOSPHERE at the table was tense. Jake concentrated on drawing Holly out, and was struck by how intently Maureen listened to her daughter's every word. She never interrupted, or even asked Holly a question, as if afraid that one word from her would shut her daughter up.

By the time Holly had finished her second helping it was seven. "Can we watch *Friends?*" she asked hopefully.

He knew the program. Apparently, Maureen did, too. She rolled her eyes before giving a reluctant nod.

"You two go ahead," he urged. "I'll just clear up these dishes."

He hadn't intended to go so far as to load the dishwasher and hand-wash the awkward Dutch oven. But when Maureen stayed behind to help, he was happy to prolong their time together.

With Holly gone from the room, Maureen relaxed visibly. She removed a clip from her thick blond hair and let it settle around her face. No makeup or glam clothes today, he noted approvingly. Still, Maureen would look classy and poised no matter what she wore. Including the jeans and white-and-blue-striped shirt she had on today.

"What made you decide to start a heli-skiing

business, of all things?'' she asked, as she rinsed the silverware and passed it to him to put in the dishwasher.

''I got hooked on skiing at an early age. During my Christmas vacations at the ranch, we'd spend every day we could on skis. Both downhill and country.''

Those were happy memories. Tainted only by the recollection of how miserable he'd felt at the end of each holiday when it was time to return to Ontario and his mother.

''But as you grew older, didn't you have any more serious ambitions than just to ski?''

''Heli-skiing is fun. It's also big business. Grizzly Peaks isn't a lazy man's diversion.''

''I never meant to imply you were lazy. But don't you worry the lifestyle you've chosen insulates you from the issues and problems of the real world?''

''What is the real world, if not snow and mountains and trees?'' Jake shook his head. ''Sometimes I think you business types are the ones with your heads up your—''

He stopped abruptly and Maureen laughed. Then she totally surprised him. ''Maybe you're right. At least partially. My perspective of life has been changing lately.''

''When I'm working out on the mountain, I can't wait to get up in the morning, and I never count the days to my next vacation. Did you feel that way about your job in Calgary?''

For a moment, her expression softened. But her answer was pure, practical Maureen. ''My job paid the bills. And Lord knows there were enough of those.''

Jake squirted dish soap into the Dutch oven, then filled it with hot water. ''I'm not suggesting anyone shirk financial obligations. I certainly never have.''

''I don't doubt it,'' she said. ''I'm sorry if I'm giving you a hard time. You're lucky you're able to make a good living doing something you love. I love the law, too. At least, I used to....''

She got that thoughtful look again, and he had to admit it did strange things to him. He'd never met anyone with her unique combination of strength and vulnerability.

''Maureen...'' He put a damp hand to her waist and was surprised when she didn't pull away. ''Tell me about it.''

He wanted to know the hopes and dreams she'd had when she was young. Clearly at least some of them had been dashed. What had happened? It wasn't just her husband's tragic death. Somehow Maureen's life had fallen offtrack before that.

''Tell you what?''

''Why you studied law in the first place. What did you think you'd be doing with your life?''

''I had no higher aspirations than to dazzle the

courts with my incredible intellect, as well as earn a ton of money.'' She grimaced. ''That's not to say I wasn't idealistic. But a few short years in our justice system ground that out of me.''

''Was it the justice system, then, that made you so cynical? Or your marriage to Rod?''

She folded her hands back on her hips. ''You think I'm cynical?''

He took one of the glasses from dinner and half filled it with water. ''What do you see?''

''A potential breeding ground for bacteria.'' She took the glass and dumped out the water before placing it upside down in the top rack of the dishwasher.

Jake laughed. ''See? You're off the charts where cynicism is concerned.'' Of course, it took one to know one. Funny that she didn't realize he was a cynic, too, behind what he hoped was an easygoing exterior.

''We're just about done here,'' she said. ''Want to watch the rest of Holly's program?''

''Honestly?'' He put his hands on her shoulders. ''Not really.''

''Jake…'' She took a step backward, but that only gained her a few centimeters. The counter prevented her from moving farther.

''Jake,'' she said again, almost as if she were pleading.

He hoped that she was, because he wanted to kiss

her in the worst way. *Kiss me, Jake,* he imagined her saying, then lowered his head obligingly.

"Stop." Maureen planted her entire hand on his face. "Jake, I'll be honest. There are some weird vibes in this room. I'm not sure what to make of them."

He pried her fingers off, one by one, undecided whether to laugh or to sulk. Never had a woman quite so ignominiously made it clear she didn't appreciate his advances.

"Do you call it weird," he asked carefully, "when a man is attracted to you?"

"Rod and I were married a long time. I haven't dated in almost two decades." She wouldn't look at him. Instead, she licked her dry lips as she struggled, for the first time since he'd met her, for something to say.

"Is it too soon, then? Since your husband's death…?"

She shook her head. "No. That's not it. I'm just… I don't know. We don't seem like the right mix."

"How can you say that when we haven't tried mixing yet? You know a few dates wouldn't hurt anything." Not to mention a few *kisses.*

"But we're business partners."

"We're not running Microsoft, Maureen. We don't have to worry about how this will look to the employees."

"That doesn't make it the smart thing to do."

"Let's drop the debate, okay? If you don't want to go out with me, all you need to do is say no."

"Oh."

"Not 'oh.' No."

"I heard you, Jake." She pulled back her hair and resecured the clip she'd removed earlier, avoiding his gaze all the while. "We *really* should be going. Holly probably has homework."

His thoughts and emotions in a scramble, he could only watch as she slipped out of his arms and headed to the living room.

Predictably, Holly kicked up a fuss when requested to turn off the set before her show was over. Still, she did as her mother asked and reluctantly followed her outside to the BMW.

Jake stood at the door to wave goodbye and hoped his smile masked his inner turmoil. He couldn't remember when a woman had tied him in knots the way Maureen Shannon managed to do.

He wasn't even certain why he continued to pursue her. She was probably right when she said it wasn't smart for them to get involved. Not because they worked together, but because of the way she made him feel.

From the beginning, his mind had warned him to keep his distance. Somehow, though, his instincts took over whenever they were together.

"Not instincts, buddy. Hormones," he corrected himself.

With the BMW out of sight, he locked his front door and then went back to the kitchen to grab a beer. Even as he popped the cap, he knew he was kidding himself.

He had plenty of experience with hormones. What drew him to Maureen was much more complicated.

And infinitely more fascinating.

CHAPTER SEVEN

TWO DAYS WENT BY WITHOUT Jake seeing Maureen. He acknowledged he had it bad when he started running to get the phone in case it was her. In his desperation, he ended up calling Cathleen.

"You've got to give me some inside information here. Help me out."

"Poor Jake." Cathleen laughed. "You're out of your depth with Maureen, aren't you." She paused while she considered. "You know what my sister needs?"

He let the suggestive opening pass. "What?"

"To get out and have some fun. Since Rod's death she's been keeping her nose to the grindstone. Actually, that's what she's been doing for *years*."

Cathleen sounded surprised, as if she'd just noticed. Hell, *he'd* figured something was wrong the first time he'd met Maureen, at Cathleen and Dylan's original engagement party an aeon ago.

"Yeah, well, that's what I had in mind. Generally I like to think my dates have *fun* when we go out together. But as I just tried to explain, Maureen won't have anything to do with that."

"So it can't be a date.... I know! Ask her to play tennis. Maureen used to be a real whiz."

Not a bad idea. Tennis wasn't a date. It was the sort of thing buddies did together. And business partners?

"And, Jake—let her win. Maureen *loves* to win."

He swung his free arm gracefully through the air, already picturing the moment he'd plant that last serve just out of reach of Maureen's racket.

"You know what, Cathleen? So do I."

"MAUREEN? JAKE'S HERE, he wants to talk to you!"

Maureen heard Cathleen call to her up the stairs of the lodge. She'd set up a minioffice in her bedroom, using a small table as a desk.

"Just a minute!" She filed her last e-mail message, then shut down her laptop. Why would Jake be dropping by? She paused at her bureau mirror to dab on a little lipstick. Maybe there was a problem with the business.

She ran lightly down the stairs and ended up in the kitchen. Abruptly, she stopped at the sight of Jake in a pair of shorts and a white T-shirt.

"Is that a tennis racket in your hand?" she asked.

"No, I'm just happy to see you."

Cathleen, drinking coffee at the kitchen table, sputtered. Maureen frowned. Evil plans were underfoot. She could just *tell*.

"Do you have a game lined up with Dylan?" But then, why had Cathleen called *her*?

"I was hoping you'd give me a match," Jake said.

"Well, I'm sorry, but my racket's in storage."

"You can borrow mine," Cathleen said quickly.

Now Maureen knew this was a setup. "I need to collect Holly from school in half an hour."

"Poppy's already in town. She was going to get her. Remember?"

Cathleen could sound so sweet sometimes. She was totally deceptive that way.

"Don't stand there with your mouth open, Maureen. Change your clothes. I'll be right back with the racket." True to her word, Cathleen took off for the basement, where she and Dylan kept most of their sporting equipment.

Maureen was left gaping at Jake. He waited patiently, obviously amused. A wild thought went through her mind. *He must really like me to have gone to all this trouble.* Then she gave herself a mental kick. *It's only tennis.*

"I haven't played in years," she said.

"Good," he replied. "I'm going to whip your butt."

JAKE DID MANAGE TO WIN the first game. The second one, too…barely. Maureen was back in form by the third, though, and left him stranded at the top of the court with a well-placed ball at the back left-hand corner.

"My game," she called, swatting the mesh of her racket. She swiveled and positioned herself to serve, knees bent, left leg in front of the right.

"Ready?" She tossed a ball in the air and raised her racket behind her.

Jake tried to focus. It was a hot day for June— felt more like July or August—and the sun was in his eyes. He really should have worn a cap....

Whack! The ball landed hard, making a hollow sound on the clay court. He hadn't even seen it coming.

"Fifteen love..."

She had the second ball in the air before he had a chance to get back into position. He caught this one, though, sending it low and long over the net. Too long. Damn.

"Out!"

Focus, Jake!

Whack!

"In."

Not on her legs this time.

He returned her next serve and ended up winning the point. But the game went to Maureen. The next one, too. *And* the next one.

"That's the set," she said, loping to the net. "Want to play another?"

He swung his racket in the air, pretending he had

another shot at that last zinger she'd flown by his left ear. "My mother said I had to be home in time for supper."

She laughed, then jumped the net. "Are you sulking?"

"Your sister forgot to mention you once played Wimbleton."

She laughed again. "I did play in university. And for a few years Rod and I had a membership at the Calgary Tennis Club."

Tennis had never been his number-one sport. So that made him feel marginally better about losing. "You have a wicked serve," he allowed.

"Really? I always thought my backhand was my best stroke."

"Backhand's good, too." With a small white towel he wiped his brow, then his hands and the handle of his racket. He was still a little out of breath and his right forearm ached. It was a good ache, though, from a hard workout. Nothing damaged.

Maureen was zipping her sister's racket inside the cover, humming softly. She looked so happy his bad mood evaporated.

"You really do like to win, don't you?" And losing wasn't so bad, he figured, when it put a smile like that on her face.

"I can't remember when I last had this much fun."

"Then we'll have to do it again."

She didn't even hesitate. "I'd like that."

AS JAKE DROVE HER BACK to the B and B, Maureen felt as if she was melting into the bucket seat of his Expedition. She was tired, a very satisfied sort of tired. Almost like that satiated feeling after making love...

She snuck a look at Jake. The expression on his face the first time she'd whizzed one of her best serves past him had been absolutely priceless. She didn't blame him for being a little ticked at losing—if the situation had been reversed, she would have been, too—but she was glad that he'd gotten over it quickly.

Too often she'd been paired with men who truly resented being bested by a woman.

Like you know who.

"Why did you stop playing?" Jake asked her. "You obviously love the sport."

"Between work and Holly, there was never time." On a few occasions she'd tried to organize games with friends, counting on Rod to stay home with the baby. But having to cancel when her husband failed to come home at the time he'd said he would was embarrassing. And she couldn't ask the nanny to stay extra hours. Not when she already felt so guilty for the long days she put in at work.

"I know how that goes," he said. "The wives of my two favorite climbing buddies had babies last year. Seems like those guys never have any free time anymore.''

"At least you still have your skiing.''

"Yes, I do. It is a job, though. When I get a hotshot who doesn't know when to call it quits, combined with the wrong weather conditions and a slope of unstable snow, I'm definitely not having fun any longer.''

Maureen frowned at the reminder of the dangers involved. "Have you ever been caught in an avalanche?''

"Not me, no, but I had to rescue a couple of my clients once.''

"Were you scared?''

"Hell, yes! Believe me, I always try to err on the side of caution when I'm out in the backcountry. Avalanches vary in size, of course, but I've seen them tear full-grown trees out by the roots. You don't want to mess with something like that.''

No, he was right. She didn't.

They were at the turnoff for the B and B. Maureen hung on to the edge of her seat as the truck jostled on the rougher road. First one wide curve to the left, then another to the right. Now the lodge was in plain view. Judging by the vehicles parked out front, everyone was home.

"Well, thanks, Jake. I really needed that.''

Before she even had her door open, his hand on her shoulder stilled her. "You know, I forgot to tell you what we were playing for. As the loser, I owe you big-time.''

"That's okay." She blinked innocently. "Winning is enough for me."

He pulled at the stubby ponytail sticking out from the back of her white cap. "I insist. I always settle my debts."

His eagerness to pay up was very suspicious. "Forget it, Jake. We never even made a wager."

"You beat me fair and square," he said. "So now I owe you dinner. Saturday night. Seven o'clock."

She might have known it. "That's very sneaky of you."

"You don't have to consider it a date."

"Don't worry. I won't." She reached out to touch the bridge of his nose. "You got a little sunburned. You should put on some cream."

He caught her hand before she could retract it. With his gaze on her eyes, he lowered his head. She just had time to close her eyes, to tilt her head, before their lips met.

His were parted and warm and she could taste the outdoors as she adjusted hers to accommodate him. A second or two of sweet, toe-curling bliss, then he pulled back, letting go of her hand and tugging her ponytail a second time.

All of a sudden Maureen was sixteen again, rediscovering the excitement that was possible from one tiny kiss. She stared at Jake's lips, still moist from touching hers. He had a beautifully shaped mouth, quite likely his best feature. Raising her gaze a little, she became mesmerized by his eyes. Swirling in those light blue pools were promises of pleasure that weakened her knees and turned her previous opinions about the future of their relationship into mush.

If one kiss can be this marvelous, think of the other possibilities....

"Tell me, Maureen. When are you moving into your new town house?"

The mundane question was a disappointment. "In about five weeks. I can hardly believe it. Between selling my house in Calgary in a flash and a new one being available so quickly, there's been almost no breathing space."

"Maybe it's a sign that this was meant to be."

Maureen knew he meant her move to Canmore, not her partnership with him. Still, she did suddenly have a sense of inevitability where he was concerned. Regardless of whether it was right or wrong, smart or insane, something was going to happen between them.

And, judging from that kiss, it was going to be very thrilling when it did.

ON SATURDAY NIGHT, MAUREEN reflected that one of the good things about moving to Canmore was that she now had an abundance of baby-sitters. Not that Holly needed sitting; still, it was nice not to have to leave her alone. Cathleen and Dylan were visiting with friends, and Harvey was whisking Poppy away for an overnight trip to Jasper, but Mick and Kelly were happy to take Holly for the evening.

"Let her stay the night," Kelly urged. "Billy and Mandy will be so tickled."

Holly was thrilled with the plan, too—so Maureen agreed she should pack a bag.

Kelly, dressed in running pants and a tank top, was waiting in the front yard with the children when they drove up at seven o'clock. All three ran to Holly and engulfed her in a smothering group hug.

"We're so glad you decided to stay overnight," Kelly said. "You and Mick are going to watch a movie with the kids while I go for a run. Later, once the little guys are in bed, we've got another movie for us adults."

Holly glowed at being grouped with the grown-ups for once. She bent low to scoop little Amanda into her arms. "You're so cute! I love your barrettes. Are they kittens?"

Amanda nodded. "Kewwy says we're going to get a kitten. Right, Kewwy?"

"Either a cat or a dog. We haven't decided which." Kelly placed a hand on her slim hip and Maureen coveted her athletic figure. *She* simply hadn't been born that way. Or was it that she wasn't willing to work as hard as Kelly did at staying fit? Nah, better to blame it on genes.

"I'll pick you up in the morning," she said when Holly stood. She longed to step forward for a good-bye hug, but Holly was already heading for the house, giving no indication that she'd heard that last remark.

"You look great, sis," Kelly said. "I like how you did your hair."

Maureen snuck a peek in the side mirror of her car. She'd tried back-combing it the way her hairdresser always did and she was pleased with the results.

"Have fun," Kelly said. "And remember, we've got Holly *for the whole night.*"

"EVERY TIME I COME HERE I order the same thing," Jake confessed once the waiter had opened their bottle of wine and left. "Black bean chowder and the cedar-planked salmon. Boring, I know, but they're just so good I can't resist."

"That's what I'll try, then." Maureen put down the menu. She was glad they'd decided to drive to Banff. Here she could relax and enjoy herself, without worrying that some busybody would report back to her sisters on her every move.

Not that their matchmaking efforts hadn't been well intentioned and, face it, a little inspired, as well. But now it was definitely time for them to butt out.

Playing tennis on Wednesday had taught her something important. She ignored an entire aspect of her personality for too long. As a teenager and young adult she'd thrived on competitive sports. But it was more than physical activity that she craved. It was everything that went with it. The competition, the camaraderie, the *fun*.

Face it. She hadn't had a social life in years. As for Jake, provided they both understood they were just enjoying each other, then where was the harm? Jake likely didn't have anything more meaningful on his mind, anyway.

Her pleasurable mood dipped a little at that thought. She immediately chastised herself. She'd be a fool to expect anything deep and meaningful with Jake. Never mind those thoughtful, probing looks he was prone to give her.

She held her glass of wine up to the candlelight. The rich garnet Shiraz seemed a fitting prelude to the pleasures that awaited her this evening. Gourmet food, interesting conversation and a dash of sexual excitement thrown in for good measure.

Jake *was* devastatingly handsome in his blue shirt and navy jacket. His eyes glowed with a seductive combination of self-assurance and admiration. Every time his gaze dipped to the v-neck of her silk blouse, she felt an anticipatory tingle all over her body.

Not that she intended to take Kelly's hint and

sleep with Jake tonight. But surely their good-night kiss would last a little longer than that first sampling he'd stolen after tennis.

That kiss. Every time she thought about it, she got a sexual rush. Was it just because she hadn't made love with a man in so long? Or was there truly something exceptional brewing between her and Jake?

He leaned forward to touch her hand briefly. "Tell me what you're thinking."

"I'm wondering if I remembered to shut the latch on the outside garbage container when I emptied the trash this afternoon."

This time it was her wrist he touched, right at the pulse point, where she'd sprayed perfume an hour ago.

"I don't believe you."

"Oh, really? Then why don't *you* tell me what I was thinking about."

He pushed aside the place setting so that he could lean even nearer to her. In a low, sexy voice he said, "You're hoping that even though this isn't a date, I'll still kiss you good-night."

His guess was so close to her actual thoughts she couldn't dissemble. In the pause while he waited for her answer, the entire restaurant seemed to go silent.

"Well." She took another sip of her wine. "Will you?"

SINCE MAUREEN HAD DRIVEN to Jake's after dropping Holly at Kelly's, her car was still parked out front when they returned to his town house from the restaurant. Jake sighed when he pulled up behind the black sedan.

"This means I can't drive you home. I was looking forward to that." He reached a hand to her shoulder. All night he'd wanted to touch her blouse. Cool silk over warm skin.

"Eager to get rid of me?"

"You noticed, huh?" He slid his hand down her arm, captured her hand. Also warm.

Although she was sitting right next to him, the dusky light made it impossible for him to judge her expression. At the restaurant there'd been no mistaking the sparks between them. But he didn't want to take anything for granted. He wasn't ready to risk another hand planted in his face.

He squeezed her fingers; she squeezed back. Surely tonight he wasn't reading the signals wrong. "Would you like a drink before you go?"

"Yes."

Which meant they ought to get out of the car. But he couldn't bring himself to stop touching her. With his free hand he caressed the side of her neck, gently turning her face toward his. Her muscles felt stiff, just a tad resistant.

"Is this okay?" he asked softly.

As soon as she nodded, he brushed back her thick

hair so he could graze his lips against the tender skin on the lobe of her ear.

It was awkward in the bucket seats of his vehicle, but when she tilted her face toward him, he did manage to kiss her. A little more intensely, and a little longer, than the first time.

"Oh, Maureen. My mind tells me we should be taking this slow, but..."

"I know." She wound both of her arms around his neck, and they were kissing again. Now he was flooded with the memory of how tantalizing her body had looked in her silk blouse and long black skirt, with that sexy, midthigh slit up the side.

He dropped his hand to her hip, then down the length of her outer thigh, searching for where the fabric separated. When he found it, he let out a small groan. Her stockings were so fine, so silky soft.... He trailed his hand down to her knee, then back up until he reached an elasticized band. Beyond that point was only her skin; it was so beautifully textured her stockings seemed coarse in comparison.

"Um, Jake?"

Did she know her voice dropped several notes whenever she spoke quietly? The effect was very, very sexy. He took a deep breath and tried to inhale a little sanity along with the air. If she said stop, he wasn't going to try to change her mind.

"Since we've agreed to take this slow," she said

shakily, "why don't we go inside and take it slow there?"

HE POURED HER A DRINK, her favorite brandy, and then put on music. Soft, seductive music. They danced with one hand on their glasses, the other on each other. The need to keep the golden liquid from spilling on the carpet was effective at keeping them from falling into each other.

Maureen had never felt so much desire.

Touch me there…and there…

She thought she might faint when he actually did, his hand skimming over her breast, over the slight swell of her abdomen, down to her thigh.

She leaned her head on his shoulder, raised her glass to her lips and ran her tongue over the sweetened rim. One brandy couldn't make her drunk, yet she'd definitely lost her sense of balance.

Jake's finger under her chin brought her mouth back to his for another kiss. Hot and wet and never ending. It seemed that there were no bones left in her body when he finished.

"Is this slow enough?" he asked.

"Oh, absolutely…"

They savored their drinks, and their dance, making them last until the CD was over. The next CD in the rack was strident jazz.

And all of a sudden, the discordant notes reminded Maureen of the reality of everyday life.

"I have to go home now, Jake."

He gave a disappointed sigh. "That wasn't what I was hoping you would say."

She could stay if she wanted. The knowledge was tantalizing. But somehow staying didn't feel right. Not yet, anyway. She tried to remember where she'd placed her purse.

"You've decided against the house breakfast special? No extra charge if you're interested."

"Oh, I can't, Jake. Not that I don't want to..."

"I understand." He took her arm and walked her to the front door. There, on the table by the closet, was her purse. She hung the strap from her shoulder, and before she could reach for the knob, he stopped her with a hug.

"Tonight was so wonderful, Maureen, every second of it. I want you to tell you—"

She covered his mouth with her hand. "Wait. Let me speak first...."

"You mean, for a change?"

"Don't be a smart-ass. What I need to say is that I don't know how tonight is going to change things between us. I'm not sure if it even *should*."

"How can it not? Maureen—"

She pressed her hand down more firmly. "My turn, remember? I'm not ready for a serious relationship. My life has been such a turmoil, and Holly is still so upset, and even Rod..."

She paused, not sure what to say about her late

husband. Still she felt his presence, their history together, as some sort of barrier to her future.

"So it'll be just sex for a while?" Jake said.

She couldn't help but laugh.

"Don't worry, Maureen. I understand what you mean. We can be cautious about this. Starting now. See how chastely I'm kissing you good-night?"

He laid his lips briefly to her forehead. "Hold on while I grab my jacket. I'm following you home."

"But that's—"

This time he put his hand on *her* mouth. "No buts. You've had your say. Now I'm having mine."

CHAPTER EIGHT

WHEN THE NOON BELL RANG on Monday, Holly ran to her locker to get her backpack.

"Want to walk to the park with us?" one of her new friends asked.

"Not today, thanks." She hoped she'd remembered her notebook. Yes. There it was. Slipping through the hallway of kids—they were all so much bigger than her!—she made her way to the exit.

One grade-eight girl deliberately slammed her elbow into her backpack as Holly passed. The grade eights were the worst, she'd discovered. It was the same in this school as at her school in Calgary. She was glad that summer holidays were starting soon. Then next fall *she* would be one of the dreaded grade eights. Only, she'd probably still be the shortest kid around....

Being short had its benefits, though. Ten minutes later, as Holly waited in the lineup at the Bagel Bites Café, she was confident that very few people in the crowded room would notice her, since she was just a kid.

Holly paid for a bagel and a pop, then found a

table in the corner and pulled out her notebook. She'd only just located her pen when Max Strongman walked in as he always did on Mondays, ordered coffee and a sandwich and even got his usual table by the fireplace.

12:15: Strongman arrives. Holly scribbled between bites of her cold bagel, then snapped the tab off her cola and took a long drink. It was nineteen minutes after twelve. Any second now…

The shop door opened. Holly picked up her pen.

12:20: Beth Gibson shows up. Acts surprised to see the mayor. He invites her to join him.

Holly couldn't believe how predictable they were. The same routine every week. Did they think people were stupid? Not that anyone in the crowded restaurant paid them any particular attention; still, most people *noticed* stuff like this, even if they didn't let on at the time.

He slides his hand up her knee. Yuck! This, too, happened every week. Predictably, Beth slipped her foot out of her high-heeled shoe and started playing footsie. *Double, triple yuck!*

Before Holly had finished her lunch, they were standing.

"I have to go to a meeting," Max was saying. "I could drop you off home on the way if you'd like."

It was so stagy Holly felt like rolling her eyes. Instead, she jotted down the time in her notebook, then shoved the pen and paper into her backpack.

Leaving her food on the table, she slipped out the door. As she unfolded her scooter, the couple came outside.

"So nice of you to offer me a ride," Beth said loudly.

Double groan!

Holly let them get down the block and around the corner before she kicked off on her scooter. Gliding over the smooth sidewalk, she covered the same distance in one-quarter the time.

They were getting into Max's Land Rover as she rounded the corner and started picking up speed. Just in front of their parking meter she pretended to lose her balance and tumbled onto the sidewalk.

Max and Beth were in the front seat already. Leaning toward each other, they snuck a kiss. And then another.

Snap! Snap! Holly got the pictures, certain that they hadn't even noticed her, then scootered quickly back to school before the afternoon bell.

EAGER TO SEE MAUREEN AGAIN, Jake suggested a tennis rematch for Monday afternoon. Maureen started out strong, but they played an extra set this time, and he won the last one, mostly thanks to physical endurance.

Or plain damn stubbornness.

"Want to go to my place for a drink?" he asked.

"I have to pick up Holly now." Maureen's

cheeks were ruddy; her neck and the top part of her chest, above her white tank top, glistened as if rubbed with body oil.

"Let's pick her up together, then you can both come over." And maybe he'd convince them to stay for dinner, too. Last night he'd taken a trout out of the freezer, so he'd be prepared if they said yes.

At three-thirty sharp, the bell rang and students flooded through the main doors. Holly emerged in the middle of a trio of girls. When she spotted Jake in the passenger seat of her mother's BMW, she broke away from the group with a smile.

"Jake? Cool! What're *you* doing here?"

"Your mom and I were playing tennis. We thought we'd drop over to my place for a snack. Sound okay?"

"Sure." She jumped into the back seat and snapped on her seat belt.

In silence, Maureen drove to the cul de sac, pausing to glance at the unit with the Sold sign out front.

"Not much longer," he said, wondering what it would be like when they were neighbors. They were still in the getting-to-know-each-other stage, but already he sensed he was exploring new territory with this woman. That he craved her company almost constantly was something novel for him. So the idea of having her on the same block was definitely appealing.

But also scary.

"Let's sit in the kitchen," he suggested once they were inside his place. He went to the fridge and snagged three colas. Holly's hand was in the air a second before he tossed her a can.

Mistake, he realized, noting Maureen's frown. She didn't like that Holly was so at home here. Obviously she considered he had no father potential. The thought was sobering, though probably correct. After all these years on his own, what did he know about kids?

Still, what did he need to know? He and Maureen were just dating, right? He poured one of the colas into a glass for Maureen, then opened a jar of salsa to have with the chips already on the table.

"So how are your classes going, Holly?"

"The pits. Except for science."

He asked her about her friends and after-school activities. Maureen sat quietly, listening, sipping at her cola and picking at the taco chips. After thirty minutes or so, she sighed. "We should be getting back to help Poppy with dinner."

"Why not eat with me," Jake offered quickly. He stood and placed a hand on Maureen's shoulder as if he could hold her against her will. "I have a rainbow trout thawing in the fridge, which I caught this spring. Do you like trout?"

Maureen placed her hand over his and he tightened his fingers, willing her to accept his invitation.

He could tell she wanted to stay, but before committing herself, she turned to her daughter.

"What do you say, Holly?"

Holly didn't answer. She was focusing on their hands. Her mother's and his. Discreetly, Maureen edged out of her seat and away from Jake's touch.

"Maybe we should just go home," Maureen said.

"Home. Definitely." Holly set her can of cola on the table with a thud, then stormed to the front door.

Maureen made to follow, then paused and waited for him. "I'm sorry, Jake. I guess I should've told her..."

That they were dating. Or thinking of dating. Or whatever the hell it was they were doing. Jake bit down on his disappointment, reminding himself that this was no one's fault. The situation was complicated. That was all.

"She'll get used to the idea." He tried to smile, but his lips felt stiff.

What if she didn't?

After they left, he knew he hadn't been honest with himself about anything to do with Maureen. This thing between them—it wasn't casual. Nor did he want it to be.

HOLLY'S COLD ANGER MADE the fifteen-minute car ride home very uncomfortable. She'd parked herself in the back seat, maximizing the space between herself and her mother. Several times Maureen started to speak, then stopped. All she could see was the side of Holly's head as her daughter gazed out the window, her body stiff, her fingers clenching the straps of her backpack.

Finally, at the top of the winding lane that led to the B and B, Maureen stopped the car and twisted round in her seat. "Tell me what you're so angry about," she said.

Holly shot her a killing glance and thrust out her jaw stubbornly.

"If something's upsetting you, we should discuss it."

No response.

"Are you concerned about Jake and me? Do you think the two of us—"

Holly opened the car door, then slammed it shut, all without moving from her seat. She whirled at her mother, high color in her cheeks. "I thought the two of you were just friends. But it's more than that, isn't it?"

"Well…um…yes, I guess…"

"Couldn't you have *told* me? Did I have to see you guys groping each other and figure it out on my own?"

"Jake's hand on my shoulder was hardly *groping*."

Holly began to tremble, and tears brightened her eyes but didn't fall. "What about *Dad*, Mom? You've forgotten all about him, haven't you? Because you never even loved him in the first place! When he went away, you *wanted* him to die!"

Pain knifed through Maureen's abdomen. "Holly, I did not—"

For the second time Holly yanked open the car door. But this time she jumped out, leaving her backpack forgotten on the floor.

Maureen lowered her window. "Holly, get back in the car!"

But her daughter was running up the lane, arms pumping, hair swinging with every stride.

Maureen scrambled out of her seat to follow. "Stop right this minute!" Her tennis shoes gripped the gravel well and she hit her stride quickly. But Holly had a good head start. When she ducked behind some trees, taking a shortcut rather than following the winding lane, Maureen gave up. Even if she caught her and, by some miracle, thought of the right thing to say, Holly wouldn't listen.

The futility of it all wiped her out as much as the sudden physical exertion. Breathless and disheartened, she turned back to the car. Now she moved as if her feet were weighted down with cement blocks. When she reached the stranded vehicle, she fell into the front seat feeling at a total loss.

Do something, Maureen. Drive the car. Park the car. Go inside and have dinner. Smile at everyone and pretend nothing's wrong.

But she couldn't even shift into gear.

She was so sick of this. Making excuses every time Holly struck out at her; pretending it didn't hurt, when of course it did! Every barb, snide comment and accusation stung like hell. Why was she always the one to blame, the scapegoat for every damn thing that had gone wrong in their family? Yes, she'd made mistakes. But so had Rod. Holly would never see that, though.

Maureen was the surviving spouse. Rod was the immortal hero. She could never, *never* compete with him now.

As she groped in her purse for some tissues, Holly's bitter words tortured her. *You never even loved him in the first place....*

That's what Holly thought, but she was wrong. In the beginning Maureen *had* loved Rod. She'd met him the month after she'd completed her undergrad degree and he'd transformed her entire world. After a lifetime of being the responsible eldest sister, of studying hard, finishing high school two years early, then starting right away in university, she'd found in Rod all the things she'd missed along the way. Handsome guys, all-night parties and wonderful, playful sex.

They'd spent almost every minute of that summer together, then Rod had accepted a two-year engineering project in Argentina. By the time he came back, she was finished her law degree, and once more ready to party. Impulsively, they'd married, and she'd become pregnant almost immediately.

Suddenly the fun was no longer in her court. Rod's love for her hadn't grown over the years. She'd tried to make their marriage work, but after a while she'd tired of caring so much and receiving so little in return. Rod had made it plain that he'd rather spend his spare time with anyone but *her*. He had his fishing buddies, his climbing buddies, his skiing buddies.

And his darling little angel. Whenever he *was* home, he lavished all his attention and affection on Holly. Maureen didn't begrudge any of that. She just wished he'd had some left over for her.

He'd complained that she nagged too much, that it wasn't fun to come home after work to a list of chores and complaints. Well, life wasn't always *fun* and she couldn't help that there were certain responsibilities. After all, he'd been just as keen as she to have a baby. And the house had been *his* idea.

Oh, stop it, Maureen! What does it matter now, anyway? What was important was that she *had* loved Rod. And it had *hurt* when he'd pushed her away. She forced herself to shift out of Park and felt the car nose forward. She braked when she realized she couldn't see anything. Tears streaming down her face had washed everything into one big blur.

Damn you, Rod! Damn you!

She wiped her eyes, her face, until the tissue

shredded in her hands, and still the tears kept coming.

A rap on her door brought her up short. Jake was peering in her window.

"Maureen? You okay? Where's Holly?"

Mortified, she averted her head so he wouldn't see her red eyes, her puffy lips. Glancing in the rearview mirror, she saw his Expedition parked right behind her. She hadn't heard him drive up.

"What the hell happened?" He opened the door, pulled her from the car and wrapped her in his arms.

His kindness was her undoing. She started crying again. No, not crying, *sobbing,* like a heartbroken toddler. Bawling so hard her stomach hurt, her chest ached; it was impossible to breathe.

She gasped for air, and no sooner had it than she burst into more sobs, made more awful, blubbery noises.

Minutes passed, maybe even half an hour. Her river of tears became a trickle, then dried up. Jake went to his truck and came back with some napkins from a fast-food joint. He mopped her up, then took her hand and somehow they started walking.

Not along the lane, but through the woods. Maureen felt becalmed in this quiet, hidden world, protected by the pine and the aspen. They wove their way along paths created by winter-foraging mule deer and ended up at the river's edge.

Jake led her to the slope-backed cedar chairs that

Dylan had built only a few months ago. The new wood was still raw and blond, but soon it would weather into a natural, streaked gray. Jake sat and pulled her to his knee.

Leaning into him, she felt like a child, or maybe just one very sad and confused woman. The angle of the sun's rays was low and long shadows emphasized every ripple on the water's surface. Closing her eyes, Maureen tried to let the sound of the river carry her spirit out of her body and her own petty problems, but nothing could erase the memory of Holly's stricken face, or the venom of her words.

Why did it hurt so much? Maureen had always known how her daughter felt. But this was the first time she'd dared to speak out.

"Holly b-blames me for everything...."

Jake brushed her hair back from her face with soothing hands. "I know."

Of course he did. Jake saw everything. She stared at her hands, balled up in her lap, still clutching the sodden napkins.

"She accused me of forgetting all about her father. She said I'd never loved him and that I *wanted* him to die on that mountain."

"Holly's just a kid. She doesn't know—"

"But it's true, Jake! A part of me *did* want him to die." She couldn't believe she'd actually said it. Every day since they'd found out about Rod, she'd seen the accusation in her daughter's eyes, but until this moment she'd never admitted it, not even to herself.

When Rod had left that last time, she'd *prayed* something terrible would happen. The plane would crash; he'd fall off a precipice....

"There's something you're not telling me, isn't there?"

Maureen stiffened and pushed herself out of his lap. How far could she really trust this man? She'd said too much already.

He stood beside her. Shoving his hands in the pockets of his jeans, he leveled his gaze at her. "Did you two have a fight before he left?"

Maureen covered her mouth. *He knew. How did he do that?*

"That's what I thought." Jake closed the distance between them, captured her hand. "Maybe you should try telling me what happened."

Maybe she should. She was surprised to realize she *did* want to tell him. That the words were more than ready to come out. "The night before Rod left we had a terrible fight. My husband asked me for a divorce."

"What?"

She was so ashamed to admit it. "He told me he didn't love me anymore. That he hadn't loved me for a long, long time."

Her voice wavered; she felt her lips tremble. "As soon as he returned from that climbing expedition he intended to file the papers." And what a slap on the face *that* would have been. After all those years of struggle, he'd planned to simply walk out on her. But it hadn't worked out that way. "Of course he *didn't* come back."

"Have you told anyone this?"

"No one."

He sighed. "Oh, Maureen."

"I decided long ago that Holly doesn't need to know about the problems between her father and me."

"But why didn't you confide in your sisters?"

She thought about that. "I'm close to them, of course. But it's different as the eldest. Cathleen and Kelly see me as someone who's always in control, who has all the answers. I couldn't admit to them that in truth my life had fallen apart even before Rod's accident. Part of it was pride. I preferred that they see me as a strong, surviving widow rather than a spurned wife."

Maureen let her face fall against the soft wool of his sweater as she thought back on some of her darkest moments.

"When I found out that Rod had died on that mountain, I tried so hard to feel sad. But all I had was anger. It was so awful, Jake. I longed to cry, to feel the things a normal widow feels.... And every time I looked at Holly, my guilt just grew heavier and heavier. He was her *father*. At least I could've grieved for that.''

"Oh, Maureen. Stop feeling something's wrong with you. That man let you down badly. Not just when he asked for a divorce but throughout your marriage, as well.''

At this moment Jake's chest was the safest place on earth. That he hadn't been repelled by all she'd told him amazed her.

"But—"

"No buts, Maureen. You had no chance to adjust to the shock of his asking you for a divorce before you were hit with another whopper. What amazes me is that you didn't suffer a total breakdown.''

Maureen reached a tentative hand to his cheek. "You've never even been married. How can you possibly know how I felt?'' Yet he did. Every word he spoke rang true in her heart.

"Lucky guesses?''

She smiled. "I'm sorry I fell apart on you, Jake. Believe me, I don't make a habit of it.''

"I know. Frankly, I think you were overdue.''

She shivered as a breeze danced across the river and over her bare arms.

Jake noticed and wrapped his arm around her shoulders. "Let's go inside. I'll make you some tea.''

His offer was tempting. She still felt so raw, and Jake had suddenly become her protector. In truth, she was afraid to face her sister and grandmother. And most of all, Holly.

"I'd rather go to your place," she confessed. Wouldn't it be wonderful to just once run away from her problems.

Jake stopped. "You sure?"

"I'm sure I want to. But I know I can't." She took one of his hands and pressed it between hers. "Thanks so much, Jake. You've really helped me put a few things into perspective."

He took a step away from her, still clinging to her hand. "I'll call you tomorrow."

"Okay." Slowly, inch by inch, they broke apart. Maureen felt alone in a way she hadn't felt in years. And he wasn't even gone yet.

"Jake?"

He turned back to her. "Yeah?"

"Thank you."

DINNER WAS LONG OVER when Maureen entered the B and B. No one was in the kitchen except Poppy, who sat sipping tea and staring out the window. For once, she didn't suggest food or drink. In fact, other than a sympathetic smile, she gave no reaction to Maureen's presence at all.

Maureen sat in the chair opposite her and folded her hands on the table. She knew she looked terrible, that Poppy could tell at a glance she'd been crying, but Poppy remained quiet.

After several long minutes, Maureen finally asked, "Did Holly come down for dinner?"

"No, but I took her up a tray. We talked a little. She'll be okay. Maybe not real soon, but eventually."

"I hope so."

"She's very like her mother. Strong, confident, resilient when facing adversity."

Wearily, Maureen covered half her face with one hand. "You think? I don't feel so resilient right now."

"Sometimes you have to touch bottom before you can push your way to the surface again."

The comment struck Maureen as wise. She glanced at Poppy, wondering if perhaps she'd been too judgmental about the older woman's presence in their lives. After all, it wasn't Poppy's fault her son had been such a loser. She of all people knew how little control a mother could have over her child's behavior at times.

"Maureen, I can imagine it's strange to have a grandmother foisted on you at this stage of your life. But I want you to be aware of something. We haven't known each other long, but I love you and your sisters with all my heart. My deepest wish is to be here for you when you need me. You're the eldest, but even you need someone to lean on now and then."

Again, Poppy was bang on with her comments. It

was difficult being the big sister all the time. Maureen laid her hand flat on the table. Tentatively, Poppy placed her hand on top. Her fingers were a little misshapen with age and arthritis, but they were still strong.

"My husband didn't love me anymore," Maureen found herself saying. "He wanted a divorce. If he hadn't died on Mount Aconcagua, that's what would've happened."

Now two people shared her secret. She was falling apart; that was what she was doing.

"Ah, Maureen. You keep too much inside. From what I hear from your sisters, your mother was like that. You're the most like her, aren't you. I can see it in the old photographs. In the eyes and the mouth. So much strength and independence, and stubbornness, too."

"My sisters would agree to the stubbornness, that's for sure." She put her hands to her temples, wishing she could stop the sorrows that kept bouncing relentlessly in her brain.

"What are you hiding from now?" Poppy asked softly.

Maureen's first impulse was to deny that she was hiding from anything. But deeper, more honest thought, told her she was. Her relationship with Holly, for one. And the newly forming relationship with Jake.

"I don't want to make the same mistakes as before,'' she said. ''Sometimes it seems that my fear paralyzes me. I want to explore what I feel for Jake. But I'm so afraid it'll turn sour. Just as it did for Rod and me.''

''But why compare the two men?''

Maureen paused. She couldn't say because they were both into extreme sports, although that was the initial similarity she'd noticed. As she'd grown to know Jake better, she'd realized any likeness was superficial. Rod was into whatever was new and exciting. He lived for those precious moments when he could feel himself teetering on the edge.

Whereas Jake didn't thrive on danger purely for the sake of it. His deep, abiding love of the mountains was reflected in his passion for skiing and climbing. But he had a healthy respect for the elements. And no wish to push the envelope, the way Rod had.

''Maybe it's not Jake I'm worried about, but me.''

''You should have more faith in yourself. And your instincts. Not just where Jake is concerned, but Holly, too. Trust your heart.''

For the first time, Maureen glimpsed a family resemblance in Poppy's aging features. Behind the lines of character and kindness were the delicate bones of her own face.

''Think I might have a little of my grandma in me, too?''

Poppy's round eyes filmed with moisture. "Maybe just a dash."

Impulsively, Maureen leaned forward and gave her a hug. "I hope so."

Poppy squeezed her in return, then pulled away to examine her face. "I'm glad to see some color back in your cheeks. Now that you're feeling better, maybe you can eat. Leftovers are in the fridge."

"I'll warm something up," Maureen promised. Once Poppy had retired to her room, Maureen laid her head on the kitchen table, too tired at the moment even to crawl upstairs to bed, let alone feed herself.

She found herself remembering Rod's funeral. How that night, after everyone had left and her sisters were sleeping—one in the extra bed in Holly's room, the other in the spare bedroom—she'd felt so alone. She'd held Rod's picture in her hand and fought an urge to smash it against the wall.

She didn't have that anger anymore. What she mainly felt was regret. Somehow she and Rod had brought out the worst in each other. And the person who had suffered the most was Holly.

CHAPTER NINE

HOLLY AND POPPY WERE HAVING breakfast together in the kitchen when Maureen came downstairs the next morning. Maureen had a residual headache from yesterday's crying, but she managed a cheerful smile. Somehow, problems *did* seem more manageable in the morning. And today, she had a game plan.

"Hello," she said. "Hope you both slept well last night."

"'Morning, Maureen. I certainly did," Poppy said.

Holly, of course, didn't reply. Maureen tried not to let it bother her. She went straight to the coffeepot, then warmed half a glass of milk in the microwave.

"I have some business in Calgary this afternoon. I wondered if you might like to take the day off school and come with me, Holly. You could have a couple of hours at the main library to research your final social studies report, then we could maybe do some shopping."

From the corner of her eye, Maureen saw her stiffen. "Why would I want to do that?"

"Well, you did mention that you couldn't find all the information you needed at the Canmore library...plus, I thought we could stop in at that coffee shop in Strathcona on our way into the city. Remember the one—"

"The Bean Scene. Dad always went there on the way to the mountains."

Holly looked amazed that her mother even knew of the place. But Maureen *had* been included on a few of those trips, although it was true that in the later years, Rod and Holly had mostly gone alone.

"Yes. I've been craving one of their homemade lemon poppy seed muffins for a long time." The microwave beeped and Maureen added the hot milk to her coffee. By the time she turned to sit at the table, Poppy's chair was vacant. Significantly, Holly still sat in hers.

"Dad loved those muffins, too," Holly mused. "But why today?"

"You don't have any tests, do you?"

"No..."

"Well, I thought we could use a little break. After...yesterday." She didn't, couldn't, go further than that, and wasn't surprised when Holly stood up from the table without saying anything else.

Still, ten minutes later while Maureen was packing papers into her briefcase, Holly came into her room.

"What'll I do while you're at the office?"

Maureen tamped down her excitement. "I should be able to finish everything while you're at the library."

"I guess it would be better than school."

"You'll still be working, Holly. Don't forget to bring a notebook to copy down your research."

"Mother. Ever heard of photocopying machines?"

Maureen gripped the handle of her briefcase. "Nevertheless, please make sure you have some paper and a pen."

Five minutes later they were on the road. Maureen resisted the temptation to pick up her cell phone and place a few calls. They were important, but business could wait the hour it would take to drive into the heart of the city.

She turned the radio to a rock station and endured the monotonous beat of several rap tunes without complaining. She could feel Holly's occasional questioning glances.

What is my mother up to now? she was undoubtedly thinking. The truth was, Maureen didn't know. She was definitely playing this minute by minute. But she had to be doing *something* right. That Holly had agreed to get in the same vehicle as her after their fight yesterday was a major accomplishment.

At an advertising break, Maureen turned the radio down. "Listen, Holly. I want to talk about Jake."

"He's pretty cool," Holly allowed. "I like him okay."

"I do, too, but so far our relationship isn't exactly serious. If it does get to that stage, I promise I'll tell you."

"Whatever."

The indifference was staged, Maureen told herself. She pushed herself to keep going.

"I know I've made mistakes in the past. And I'm sorry for them. You're the most important thing in the world to me."

"Except for work, you mean."

That stung, as it was meant to. "I used to think your father was the one who let you down by making plans and then changing them at the last minute when he got an opportunity from one of his buddies to do something fun, like mountain climbing or bungie jumping."

Maureen paused. She was worried that if she made this too long, Holly would tune her out. But there was so much to say, if her daughter would only listen.

"But recently I've been realizing that my long hours at work were letting you down, too. I should've been there more than I was." Even knowing Holly preferred Rod's company, she should've *been there*.

Holly said nothing in reply. When the commercial break was over she jacked up the radio volume again. Maureen snatched a glance at her daughter's still profile. What was she thinking behind that quiet facade?

By the time they'd stopped for muffins and then driven downtown it was eleven. Maureen turned off the Tenth Street bridge onto Fifth Avenue. Downtown was busier than ever these days. The tall buildings lining the streets blocked out the summer sunshine and the intense traffic required Maureen to focus on the road. She dropped Holly off at the main entrance to the library.

"I'll pick you up in two hours," she said. "Phone me on my cell if you have any problems."

"Okay, Mom. Thanks for the ride."

The car behind her honked. Maureen took off as soon as Holly was safely on the sidewalk. She smiled despite the look of irritation the driver from behind gave her.

Her daughter had thanked her for the ride. It was such a little thing that she couldn't believe she was so happy. But it was a baby step in the right direction.

MAUREEN AND HOLLY WERE BACK at the B and B around five o'clock. By any standard, the day had been successful. Maureen had accomplished several solid hours of work and Holly had rounded out the research for her project. After, they'd fit in shopping at the Eaton's Centre, where Holly bought new shoes and a tube of flavored lip gloss, an ultrasweet watermelon-peach combination. Maureen didn't care. Her daughter was speaking to her again.

Cathleen met them at the kitchen door. Dressed in her jeans and work boots, she'd obviously just returned from riding her quarter horse, Cascade. She oohed and aahed appropriately over Holly's purchases. When the young girl escaped to her bedroom, probably to try her new shoes on again and admire herself in the full-length mirror, Cathleen pulled Maureen aside.

"Everything okay? Holly seems happy."

"Yeah. We're on an upward turn, I think." Although the battle was far from over.

"Want a glass of iced tea?" Cathleen offered on her way to the fridge. "We won't be eating for a couple of hours. Poppy's run into town to get some cilantro for fajitas. Really, she should have her own garden. I've talked to Jake about it and he's promised to dig a patch in the backyard for her."

Cathleen tossed her hair over her shoulders. "By the way, Jake called about an hour ago."

"Oh?" Maureen reached for the glass of iced tea and tried to drink as if nothing special had just been said.

Cathleen took the phone off the console and sat

it on the table next to her sister. "I guess you'll be wanting to call him back."

"In a minute."

"You're not fooling me for an instant. I can see how eager you are to dial those seven special digits. Bet you have them memorized already, don't you?"

"Of course I do. We're business partners, remember?"

"Uh-huh." Cathleen downed her iced tea in one long swallow. "I'm going up to take a shower. If Dylan comes in—" she raised her dark brows suggestively "—tell him where to find me."

Maureen rolled her eyes. "You two are disgusting, you know that?"

But of course she didn't find her sister and her new husband disgusting at all. They were in love and in lust, and Maureen had to admit she was just the tiniest bit jealous. Because, given a chance, she'd love to lather up Jake....

Stop thinking that way!

She did. But it was difficult. As soon as Cathleen was out of sight, she dialed Jake's number. He picked up on the second ring.

"Maureen?"

She loved that he answered with her name. "I just got back from Calgary and Cathleen told me you'd phoned."

"How are you feeling today?"

"Okay. Better."

"That's good. I—oh, hell, this is hard over the phone." He paused a moment. "How's Holly?"

"She's better, too. We went to Calgary together today. After the things she said yesterday, I was amazed she would even get in the same car with me."

"Maybe she regrets her outburst. Kids can find it hard to apologize. Especially to their parents."

"Yes, that's true." She hoped he was right. "Would you like to come by for coffee and dessert later? I notice Poppy baked cookies this afternoon. They look pretty scrumptious...."

How badly she wanted him to say yes scared her. His five-second pause felt like five minutes.

"Sure. That would be great. Around seven-thirty, okay?"

Hanging up the phone, she admitted to a feeling of disappointment about their conversation. Not that Jake had said anything wrong; it was more the tone of his voice. And the fact that he hadn't jumped on her invitation to come over.

Maureen, she chided herself. She was being a pessimist again. Maybe he'd paused because he'd made other plans and was deciding whether or not he could duck out of them.

This man had been trying to date her for weeks. Of course he wanted to see her tonight.

JAKE FELT LIKE A CAD as he hung up the phone. Hearing Maureen's invitation, his first instinct had been to come up with an excuse. That impulse embarrassed him.

Her revelations last night had confirmed his impressions about her marriage and her relationship with her child. From their first meeting, he'd sensed something had been off-kilter between her and her husband. But he'd never have guessed that Rod had told her he wanted a divorce just before leaving on that ill-fated climbing expedition.

Given the state of their marriage, probably Maureen's pride had been more wounded than her heart. Still, she'd hurt and she'd kept the pain to herself until last night, when she'd told *him*. He was blown away that she'd trusted him enough to open up her heart that way. Part of him was honored. The other part was scared to death.

He was a thirty-eight-year-old man, pretty much used to fending for himself. Was he even capable of a long-term relationship with Maureen? She was a woman with exacting standards, one who'd been disappointed in her first husband and might be even more critical of the second....

And she came with a built-in daughter. Was he up to that responsibility, too? He honestly didn't know. He *liked* Holly. Despite her moods, she was a bright kid, and her usually well-disguised vulnerability brought out some latent streak of protectiveness he hadn't known he possessed.

But did he want to be her dad, responsible for vetting her dating choices, helping her map her future, not to mention all the small day-to-day stuff, which he frankly had no clue about.

You're getting ahead of yourself, man. You and Maureen are just at the beginning stages....

Jake shook his head, knowing he was kidding himself. The usual rules didn't apply anymore. They hadn't had an official date, let alone slept together, yet last night Maureen had fallen into the deep end and he'd jumped in right after her. Now it was too late to have any feelings about holding back or moving slowly.

And yet, he did.

CHAPTER TEN

"POPPY, YOU'RE THE BEST cook in the whole world," Holly declared after finishing her third fajita.

"Fresh cilantro makes the difference," the chef said modestly. "Now, if I can leave cleanup to the rest of you, I promised Harvey I would meet him at eight and I don't want to be late. He said he has something important to talk about."

"Ah!" Cathleen raised her eyebrows. "Will you give us three guesses, Poppy?"

Her answer was a flick from one of the ties on Poppy's apron. "Hush with you!"

Ten minutes later, their grandmother was out the door, minus the apron and fresh lipstick gleaming on her mouth. Stacking plates into the dishwasher, Maureen consulted Cathleen and Dylan. "Mind if we wait for coffee and dessert until Jake gets here?"

"That might be his truck right now," Dylan said.

Maureen went out on the porch and was rewarded with a view of Jake's Expedition pulling up next to her BMW. Behind him, dust from the dry dirt road still hung in the air like a low-lying cloud. She ran down the stairs and over the patchy grass toward him.

Jake stepped out from the driver's seat. Jeans and a forest-green corduroy shirt showcased his long legs and muscular chest.

"Hi there," she said, reaching out to adjust the collar of his shirt.

"Maureen. You're looking good."

"You, too…" She glanced back at the lodge, well aware that this might be their only opportunity to talk privately all night. "I was thinking, since I lost that last set on Monday, it's my turn to pay up. How about dinner on Friday?"

Jake seemed a little taken aback, and she immediately felt embarrassed. Why had she blurted out the invitation? They'd barely had time to say hello….

"Um, sure. That sounds great." He pushed his hands into the pockets of his jeans and Maureen stepped back from him.

"I didn't mean—"

"Jake! Get in here! Coffee's brewed and we have fresh cookies." Dylan was standing on the porch.

A second later the screen door slammed as Cathleen rushed out and wrapped her arm around her husband's waist. "Oh, shut up," she said. "Can't you see Jake and Maureen are talking?"

Now Maureen was truly mortified. What Cathleen

wasn't, and could never be, was *subtle*. But at least Jake was now smiling.

"Coffee sounds fine," he said. He held out his arm for her to go ahead.

They ended up gathering in the study, Holly included. Cathleen handed out mugs and set the cookies on a low table in front of the fireplace, where an arrangement of flowers had been placed for the summer season.

"Mom?" Holly held out her empty mug as Maureen made the rounds with the coffeepot.

Maureen's first instinct was to say no, then she thought, was it really worth a fight? She filled Holly's mug without a word and forced back a smile at the look of glee on her daughter's face.

She went to Jake last. He was standing by the fireplace, his stance wide and expression tense.

"Coffee?"

"Thanks."

While she poured, he put a hand to her waist. The small touch gave her a huge rush of relief. Why was she being so sensitive? Everything was fine.

When Jake's cup was full, Maureen set the carafe back on the table, then took a seat next to Holly. Her daughter didn't seem to have noticed the little moment between her and Jake. She was too busy doctoring her cup of coffee with sugar and cream. Maureen tried not to take note of how much of both she was adding to the brew.

"How's the ranching business?" Jake asked his cousin.

"Not bad. The Triple T is a good place to work. Not the same as my own spread, of course." He glanced at his wife as he heaved a sigh. "But that's an old story."

"I had lunch with Harvey today," Jake said. "He tells me that many of the preliminary hurdles to Strongman's development plans have already been cleared. This is going to happen much sooner than we figured."

Dylan dropped his head in his hands. "The oil wells were bad enough. When those cute little vacation villas start going up, my father will be rolling in his grave."

"Too bad he couldn't roll out of his grave for fifteen minutes and draw up a proper will," Maureen said.

"Mo-om!"

"I'm sorry to be blunt, but it's true. This is what happens when people don't take the time to get their legal affairs in order."

"Well, it's obviously too late for us to do anything about that now," Jake pointed out. "And it's worse than just vacation homes, Dylan. Max has a golf course planned, as well."

Cathleen groaned. "Maybe town council won't give him the approvals."

"Fat chance, when Max has handpicked the man who'll probably be our next mayor," Dylan said.

"And he'll have Alderwoman Beth Gibson's support, too," Holly said.

"What?" Maureen drew back in her seat to eye her daughter, surprised that Holly even knew Beth was an alderwoman, let alone how she might stand on any one particular issue. Holly had studied local government last year at school. Clearly she'd put what she'd learned to use.

"Why are you so sure Beth will support Max's plan?" Jake asked.

"Well, she's his girlfriend, isn't she?" Holly colored slightly. "I mean, it's kind of obvious."

"Are you talking about an affair?" Jake sounded as stunned as Maureen felt. "Beth's been married a long time. Her husband works for Parks Canada. They have two grown sons...."

All of which meant nothing, Maureen realized. "What makes you say something's going on with Max and Beth?"

Her daughter squirmed against the back of the sofa. "I just noticed them together, that's all. I saw him kiss her. And she kissed him back."

"Where did you see them?" Maureen persisted.

"Well, I was at the Bagel Bites Café for lunch one day...." She glanced sideways at Maureen, who hadn't known her daughter was leaving the school premises at noon hour. Maureen kept her mouth closed, saving that lecture for another time.

"I have pictures if you don't believe me."

"You do?" Maureen was stunned.

"Hang on a minute." Holly disappeared out the door and came back carrying a notebook. She opened it carefully, then removed a couple of photographs. "They didn't work out great...probably because it was darker in the car than on the street. But you can still tell that they're kissing."

"I knew it!" Cathleen said, shooting a triumphant glance at her husband.

"Good heavens." Maureen took the photo over to a lamp so she could examine it.

"How could Beth be so stupid?" Dylan asked in disgust. "Can any of you women explain Strongman's appeal to me?"

"Good looks, wealth, power." Cathleen ticked the attributes off on her fingers. "It's not unthinkable, Dylan. Especially when you consider the kind of money Max has made from those oil wells."

"If this relationship of theirs is serious, Beth's support may well sway the town council," Maureen conceded.

"Even worse," Dylan pointed out, "Beth's life could be in danger. I still can't figure that woman out. Didn't she see how Strongman treated my mother?"

"Maybe she hopes he's changed. Or that she'll

be the one to change him," Maureen said. "In my law practice I've met plenty of women who talked that way."

Holly reached for a chocolate chip cookie, drawing Maureen's attention back to her. "As for you, young lady, I hope Strongman didn't notice you spying on him."

"I wasn't spying. I just happened to be in the same restaurant at the same time."

"And just happened to have a camera on you, as well? Holly, you've got to be careful. If he's guilty of half the things the people in this room suspect he is, Max Strongman is dangerous. If he catches you following him around…especially if he saw you taking pictures, you could be in deep trouble."

"Oh, Mom."

"She's right," Dylan said. "You stay away from Max Strongman. He's very bad news."

And what about Beth Gibson? Maureen wondered. Just how involved was she in Max's schemes? And to think she'd given that woman a commission on the purchase of her new home!

BY FRIDAY MORNING, Jake could no longer deny that his feelings had somehow changed. As the hours leading up to his dinner date with Maureen passed, his anxiety increased. He didn't want to go.

"Why?" he asked his mirrored image as he fought with the unaccustomed tie around his neck.

The blasted thing wouldn't lie flat. Finally, he tossed it on his bed and undid the top button of his shirt. The release of pressure from around his neck felt great. He wished it could be as simple to ease the fear constricting his heart.

So call and cancel. Tell her you're feeling sick. She'll get the picture.

But he didn't have the nerve to do that. At last, Jake swore and got into his truck. He was convinced he was the biggest chump in the world. That the upcoming evening was going to be the most painful he'd ever spent.

And then he saw Maureen sitting in one of the willow chairs on the front veranda of the B and B. And he was slam-dunk infatuated again. Excitement surged through his veins at the sight of her.

She was talking with Poppy, but when he pulled up she stood and headed in his direction. Her legs seemed to go on forever in a pair of white cotton pants, and her scoop-necked pink sweater allowed a tantalizing peek at her generous cleavage. More than her great figure, he admired the confidence of her stride, her lack of self-consciousness as she pushed her thick blond hair back.

She turned to wave at Poppy and then bent to give Kip, Cathleen's golden retriever, a farewell pat.

"Have fun!" Poppy called out.

Jake barely heard her. He opened the passenger door for Maureen and wondered what had happened to all the oxygen in the air. There had been plenty just five minutes ago.

"I hope you don't mind that I was the one who suggested this dinner," Maureen said as they drove away.

"Of course not," he lied. Or was it a lie? Suddenly, their dinner struck him as a terrific idea. Only, he could have gladly skipped the restaurant and gone straight to his place.

Jake could hardly string together a proper sentence during the ride into Canmore. Again he attributed it to just hormones out of control, and that it was wrong for him to be acting this way, but he couldn't help it. Less than an hour ago, he'd thought of a million reasons their relationship wouldn't work out. And now he was wishing for nothing more than to get this woman into his bed.

Talk about superficial...

"Are you okay, Jake?"

See? She'd already noticed something was different. He'd never make it through the evening. And he didn't have to. He could claim he was sick or had a serious problem to do with his heli-skiing business. She'd understand. Or at least pretend to.

"I'm fine." He'd be all right at the restaurant, surely. Once they were surrounded by people, his emotions would settle down. The two of them could enjoy a pleasant meal together and then he'd take her home.

Maureen had booked reservations at a Mexican eatery. Not cozy and intimate, but friendly and up-beat. The waiter led them to a table in the center of the room. Out in full view. This was a good thing.

Yet touching her remained irresistible. A hand on the small of her back as they walked to the table; brushing his fingers over hers as he pointed out an item of interest on the menu.

They ordered margaritas—lime with no salt—and then he asked after Holly.

"Dylan and Cathleen invited her along with them to see a movie in Calgary. She was thrilled." Maureen smiled, then leaned over the table to play with her place setting.

Jake took undeniable pleasure in noticing the way her breasts moved beneath her sweater. Was it getting hotter in here, or was it just him? Their drinks arrived, and he guzzled half of his in mere seconds.

"Jake, you *are* acting strange. What is it?"

"Frankly, since the minute I saw you in that sweater, I've been going crazy. I'm sorry to sound like a horny teenager, but that's the plain truth."

Maureen fingered the neckline. "I told Cathleen it was too revealing. Besides, I'll probably stretch it out so much she'll never be able to wear it again."

He groaned and Maureen laughed.

"If that's the way you feel, why don't we just go to your place. The margaritas here are good, but we can try the food another day."

THEY WERE ONLY JUST INSIDE the front door when Jake reached out to kiss her. Maureen wasn't surprised. His passion had shown in his eyes since the minute he'd picked her up.

No, what surprised her was how instantly she responded. When he lowered his head to kiss her breasts through her sweater, then ran his tongue along the valley of her cleavage, she was suffused with pleasure. Jake moaned and pulled her sweater over her head, and she reached back to undo the clasp of her bra.

As he took the ample weight of her breasts in his hands, she boldly cupped her hand over the arousal in his trousers. He *did* want her. Oh, he did! She unbuckled his belt, then groaned when she couldn't get the damn zipper to budge. He paused to tug it down himself, then removed a foil package from his pocket.

Birth control. She was relieved to see that Jake was taking care of things—she certainly hadn't. But then, she hadn't really expected they would go this far tonight.

Not that she wanted to stop.

They were naked now, and he had her pinned against the front door.

"Maureen."

She *did* love the way he said her name.

"Jake... Upstairs...?"

"I...can't...wait."

And suddenly she couldn't, either. She opened to him, welcoming his deep, powerful thrusts. Her orgasm came from nowhere. It exploded all at once, turning her wild.

She used her hands to bring him closer, tilting her pelvis up to meet him. A sheen of sweat glued their bodies together as they slipped to the floor.

The discomfort of the cold, hard tiles faded under the next wave of pleasure.

They clung together for a long moment, then Jake kissed her on her temple. "This isn't exactly comfortable. Let me take you upstairs."

He picked her up as if she were a child, carrying her up the stairs, then setting her gently on his bed—which was neatly made this time, sheets taut, pillows fluffed and correctly positioned.

"Let's try this again," he murmured against her cheek. For their second time Jake took each step of the mating ritual so slowly and performed it so tenderly any woman would have been hard-pressed to find a flaw.

"That was...good," Jake said later.

"Yes—it was." She wasn't surprised to have discovered that Jake was a lusty, no-holds-barred kind of lover. The amazing thing was that apparently she was, too. What a strange revelation for a thirty-three-year-old woman with a marriage of fourteen years under her belt.

Perhaps it was only natural that her lovemaking

with Rod had fallen into a pattern over the years. They'd been more passionate at the early stages of their relationship. But never like *this*....

She rolled over to face her lover. Jake was on his back, staring at the ceiling. She could hear his still-rapid breathing. And sensed a tension she'd noticed earlier.

Something was different. Not just tonight, but the past few days. His unbridled lust had camouflaged the problems at the beginning of the evening. Now, as their hormones plateaued, she couldn't kid herself anymore.

He wanted out. Even as his hand glided over the skin of her arm, she knew she was right. His feelings for her had changed. Maybe it was a result of the confession she'd made about her marriage, or maybe it was because he was afraid to take on a woman with a half-grown child.

But Jake was suffering from cold feet. And what was worse, she'd sensed it from the beginning of their date, and *still* she'd slept with him.

"Um, Maureen, are you on the pill?"

"Fine time to ask that question."

"It's just that condoms aren't always one hundred percent effective, and I thought that if you weren't on the pill it might be a good idea to use a spermicide...."

She pulled away and left the bed. Being practical about birth control and safe sex was a good thing.

But Jake's timing—it really sucked. Remembering her clothes were still at the front door, she grabbed at the robe strewn over his chair.

"Where are you going?"

Good question. Despite the fact that she'd asked him for this date, he'd picked her up. She didn't have a car. Well, she'd worry about that later. Right now she just *had* to get dressed. She ran lightly down the stairs, and at the foyer gladly let the robe fall to the floor. It smelled too much of *him.* Of his soap, his skin.

She brushed a hand through the tangle of clothing and found her underwear. Just as she was doing up the catch on her bra, Jake appeared at the top of the stairs. Naked.

Well, of course he was naked. She had his robe. She tossed it to him, and it fell in a puddle halfway between them. After a brief hesitation, he stepped down to get it.

By then she had her pants on. She found her sweater next and cursed it silently. *All your fault...* But then it wasn't fair to blame an inanimate object for her own lack of control.

"I'm sorry. Obviously we should've discussed this earlier. I just thought it would be smart to be prepared. You know. For next time."

Jake, damn him, was looking at the carpeted stairs. Not once did he raise his eyes to hers while he spoke. "I'm not sure I see the point," she said. "There isn't going to be a next time, is there?"

He blanched. "I know I was too... That first time I should've..."

"I'm not talking about your *technique,* Jake."

He descended a few more steps, then sat so he was at eye level. "Then what is it that has you so angry? Excuse me if I'm being dense here."

His tone was sincere; she didn't think he was mocking her. But all of a sudden she realized she didn't know *what* the point *was.* Just that she felt like sitting down on the floor and bawling like a heartbroken toddler for the second time in a week.

Because he didn't love her. He'd taken her to bed, so he was obviously attracted to her. But his feelings went no deeper. He hadn't made even one tender comment after their lovemaking. She'd poured out her soul to this man, made love to him more passionately than she ever had with Rod, and all he could manage was a clinical question about birth control.

Why had she felt there was something special about him? That he was someone she could depend upon, confide in?

The answer hit her hard. The problem wasn't Jake. It was her. She'd encountered this same problem with Rod, and what it all boiled down to was that she wasn't the sort of woman men wanted to protect and look after. Jake had liked her when she was strong and independent. It was only when she'd revealed her vulnerabilities that he'd pulled away.

Well, if he liked her tough, she'd be tough.

"There isn't much to discuss, Jake. I need a ride home. You have a car. Would you mind?"

That wasn't a flash of hurt she saw in his eyes. It looked more like relief. He couldn't believe he was getting rid of her so easily.

JAKE HADN'T QUITE BROUGHT his truck to a standstill when Maureen opened the door.

"Thanks for the ride."

"Wait, Maureen—"

The door slammed, and she was gone. He watched her run for the side door, heard Kip's welcoming barks, then saw the lights snap on in the kitchen window.

Should he go after her? She was alone, he knew, since Poppy's Tracker was missing and the others were still at the movie in Calgary.

But she'd refused to listen to him at his place, and on the drive here, so what good would it do? Besides, he had no clue what to say to her.

True, he'd been suffering from a case of cold feet. But it wasn't until he was holding her in his arms, after they'd made love, that he'd known why. He'd fallen so totally in love with this woman that he was scared witless.

What was especially frightening was that it had

never happened to him before. His past held a series of short-term relationships with women he'd chosen because he found them safe. But Maureen was different. And so he'd panicked, and hurt her badly.

And he had no idea how to make amends.

He folded his arms over the steering wheel and craned his neck to see upstairs. A light went on. He pictured Maureen standing in the center of her bedroom. What would she do?

She'd take a shower. Use all the hot water and soap it took to wash every last trace of their lovemaking from her body.

The idea was so painful he had to get away. He jerked the truck into drive and heard his tires spit out gravel as he headed toward home.

CHAPTER ELEVEN

"WATCH THAT BOX, PLEASE! My computer's in there." Maureen followed the mover nervously, wincing as he banged the corner of the cardboard carton against the staircase railing.

"Sorry, ma'am."

"Careful not to trip." She trailed him up the stairs, trying to smooth out the canvas drop cloths placed over the main traffic areas. The relentless back-and-forth between the van and house had bunched the sheets to the extent that Maureen was more worried about injuries and lawsuits than dirty prints on the newly installed carpet.

"Where did you say you wanted this?" he asked.

"Master bedroom." There was an alcove by the big bay window, where she intended to set up her desk. She'd had the wiring installed for cable and an extra phone line so that she could connect to the Internet, plus have her own separate business number.

Taking on a limited amount of local legal work had been playing at the back of her mind for some time now. It made sense, given that Holly was mostly in school, and her partnership in the heli-skiing business demanded so little of her.

Thank heavens. Because having to deal with Jake on a regular basis would probably have killed her. As it was, they hadn't spoken in more than four weeks. Spring had become summer. School had let out for the annual two-month break.

"On the desk here?"

"Yes. Fine." Maureen sank onto the bare box spring and mattress and watched the man ease the cardboard box down on the scarred oak table, which had once belonged to her mother.

She'd made a lot of mistakes in her life, but never one she was ashamed of. Her relationship with Jake was the exception. Sleeping with him had been re-grettable, but what really caused her to squirm late at night was remembering when she'd cried in his arms, dumping out her most private secrets and in-securities.

With hindsight, she could view her behavior in only one way. Pathetic. Up until that point Jake had probably seen her the way others did: as a reason-ably intelligent, confident and capable woman. Be-hind that facade, however, was a woefully inade-quate wife and mother.

No wonder he'd felt compelled to back away from her. Too bad he hadn't drawn the line at sleeping with her first.

To really complicate matters, his comments about

birth control had started her thinking about pregnancy. Of course the chances were remote, since they'd used condoms. Still, the slight possibility had lived until the first day of her next period.

Gazing at the familiar tinge of pink on the expected day, she'd felt a subtle sense of sadness. Which was about the craziest reaction she ever could have expected from herself.

"Are you okay, Maureen? You look flushed." Kelly came breezing up the stairs, carrying a glass sculpture that Maureen had refused to allow the movers to touch. Carefully, she set it on one of the night tables, then pressed a hand to Maureen's forehead.

"This move has been making you crazy. You need to slow down. Who cares if the unpacking takes an extra week or two. You and Holly have lots of time to settle, and Cathleen and I'll help whenever we can."

"I'm fine. Maybe I took the stairs a bit too quickly last time." Maureen stood to admire the sculpture. It was a hand-blown abstract piece she'd picked up on a business trip to Quebec City several years ago. She adjusted the angle at which it sat, so that it caught the light from the big bay window. That was better.

"Ma'am?" a voice hollered from the front door. "Where do you want the entertainment unit?"

"Living room, please." She grimaced at her sister. "This town house is so much smaller than our house in Mount Royal. Thank heavens there's a basement, at least."

"Well, if you have any stuff you want to get rid of, check with Mick and me first. You have great taste in furniture." Kelly ran her hand over a chintz chaise longue in the corner of the room.

And lousy taste in men, Maureen silently added. It occurred to her that perhaps the blame wasn't all hers. Her well-meaning, but interfering sisters had supposedly handpicked Jake Hartman for her. In a year or two, when this fiasco was completely behind her, she intended to call them to task about that. Right now, the topic was still too painful to broach.

"I have a few of your houseplants in the car," Kelly said. "Where should I put them?"

"On the kitchen floor for now." Maureen followed her out of the room. In the hall she noticed Holly's bedroom door was closed.

The previous owners had allowed them access a week early and Dylan had gone ahead and torn down the wall between the two small bedrooms to make one larger room. Maureen gathered that Jake had helped, too, but when she'd asked, Dylan had been charmingly evasive.

Once the wall was gone, she'd had the room painted and had ordered new carpeting. She'd hoped Holly would get excited by the project, and had planned to give her daughter a free hand in the decorating, but Holly had resisted the move.

"I don't want to go. Why can't we stay here?"

"Because Dylan and Cathleen need the revenue from renting out our rooms."

"Can't you afford their usual rate?"

"That isn't the point."

Now Maureen knocked on her daughter's door. Hearing no answer, she twisted the knob and pushed inside. Holly was sitting on the floor next to a stack of cardboard boxes.

Annoyed that her daughter was hiding out while everyone else worked, she was about to make a sharp comment. Then she noticed the fine red dots at the corner of Holly's right eye. Always a sign that she'd been crying.

With a real effort, she tried to see the day from her daughter's vantage point. Maybe staying at the B and B had given Holly the illusion that they were on an extended holiday. Settling into this town house made their relocation from Calgary permanent. And maybe Holly felt that she was being distanced from her memories of her father.

"Moving into a new place is strange, isn't it?"

Holly said nothing.

"It'll be different here," Maureen acknowledged. "In the old place I could always picture your dad grabbing a snack at the fridge, or sitting on the couch by the TV. We won't have that now."

Holly pressed her lips together and her eyes flooded.

Bittersweet pain pierced Maureen in the heart. She dropped to the floor and curled her arms around her daughter. Holly didn't lean into her, but she didn't push away, either.

"Just because we moved doesn't mean we're going to forget about Dad, sweetie. We'll put up all our family photos, and we've still got the videos, right?"

Holly hiccuped, swallowing a sob. Maureen rested her cheek on the top of Holly's head and drank in the citrus scent of her daughter's shampoo.

"I miss Daddy." With Holly's words, the pent-up tears burst out. "I miss him so much."

This was the first time her daughter had shared her pain, and Maureen wanted desperately to offer some kind of advice. She tightened her hold and struggled to find the magical words that would help Holly.

But she came up with nothing.

"Of course you miss him" was all she could say, before lapsing into a frustrated silence. She thought about the time Holly was in grade one and an older child had told her she was so short she would probably be a midget.

Holly hadn't known what a midget was, but she'd recognized the meanness in the epithet.

Maureen hadn't been able to ease the sting from

that encounter, any more than she was able to deal with this. Why was she so hopelessly inadequate at helping her daughter weather life's tougher challenges? Other mothers, she was quite certain, would have known instinctively the right thing to say.

THE MOVERS WERE GONE by three o'clock. Maureen stood in the kitchen, surrounded by boxes, and thought how odd it was that a whole life had been compressed into a truckload of boxes and moved elsewhere in less than eight hours.

Stranger still was how a bunch of rooms practically crammed with furniture and plants could seem so empty and feel so cold.

Holly was in her room, listening to CDs. Her stereo had been among the first of the belongings Maureen had unpacked after setting up her own computer. Cathleen had found the clean sheets and made up the beds. Kelly had put a casserole in the fridge and paper plates and plastic cutlery on the kitchen counter.

Thanks to her sisters, she and Holly would make it through the night. But what about the weeks, the months, the years, to come?

Self-pity and depression were indulgences Maureen did her best to avoid. But today, somehow, both were tempting. She slid to the tile floor, her back pressed against the fridge, and wondered if it was too early to break open the bottle of celebratory wine her real estate agent had dropped off that morning along with the double set of house keys.

"Congratulations!" Beth Gibson had said. "I hope you'll be very happy in your new home."

Maureen hadn't invited her to stay, not with movers traipsing in and out every few seconds. But she'd thanked her for the wine.

"How are your sons?" she'd asked, standing to the side of the door so one of the movers could get past.

"The eldest works in Toronto. Advertising." She smiled proudly. "And my youngest is doing well in university."

"Having them gone must be hard. How does Alan feel about it?" She didn't know why she'd brought up Beth's husband. Maybe just to see her reaction.

But there was no flicker of guilt or secrecy as she answered, "Oh, Alan misses them—we both do. But we're busy with our work, and that helps."

Sleeping with Max Strongman must help, too. Maureen didn't know what disgusted her more. That Beth was probably cheating on her husband. Or that she'd chosen a man like Strongman to do it with.

The doorbell rang. Maureen checked the time on the stove. Almost four. Where had the past hour disappeared to? Wiping her grubby hands on her jeans as she walked, she went to see who it was.

Jake was on the front stoop when she opened the door. Maureen hated the way her entire system went into overdrive at the sight of him. He had a cloth-covered basket in his hands and a tentative expression on his face.

"Hi, Maureen. Welcome to the neighborhood. I baked some muffins."

She was ready to slam the door, but the muffins were her undoing. She could not imagine Jake Hartman at a task as domestic as baking. Opening the door wider, she let him in.

"I would've offered to help with the move, but I just got back from a trip to Calgary to pick up those new linens I'd ordered for the lodge."

"That's good." She knew her words sounded wooden. She couldn't help it. Inviting him in had been a mistake. They had nothing to talk about. Besides, with boxes everywhere, she couldn't ask him to sit, or even offer a coffee to go with the muffins.

Not that she had any intention of doing either. She wanted him gone, the sooner the better.

He passed her the basket, which was warm. When she lifted the corner of the napkin, out wafted a delicious apple-cinnamon aroma. "Did you really make these yourself?"

"Yup. First time I ever baked anything. You know, I might just do it again. It was kind of fun."

The grin he gave her was almost endearing. She had to force her heart to harden against him.

"Go ahead," he urged. "Give 'em a try."

She selected one and held it up for inspection. It was oddly shaped.

"The oven heat was too low," Jake explained. "You see, the dough rises faster than it cooks and so it ends up in that peculiar cone shape. And when you break into one, you'll see these air tunnels. That's because I overmixed...you know, when I added the dry ingredients to the wet."

Maureen clamped her mouth shut. He'd not only baked; he'd analyzed the results afterward. This was absolutely priceless.

"Don't worry." Jake looked offended. "They still taste good."

"Oh, I'm sure they do." She had to take a bite then, even though she was afraid she would choke from holding back her laughter.

She nibbled, then smiled. "Yes. Very delicious. I'm sure Holly will love them."

"Is she here?"

Maureen glanced toward the stairs. "In her room, listening to music. Can't you hear the pounding bass? Thanks, by the way, for helping Dylan with that wall. Her room looks great now. When she gets over sulking because I wouldn't agree to stay at the B and B, she'll love it."

"Oh, that wall was nothing to take down," Jake said, confirming her suspicion about his involvement.

"Well, thanks, anyway." She put her hand on the

door frame, signaling he should leave. But all Jake did was take a step closer and lower his voice.

"I've missed you, Maureen. I haven't seen you in weeks."

"Correct me if I'm wrong, but wasn't that what you wanted the last time we went out?"

He closed his eyes and winced. "I've tried to apologize for that night. I was a real jerk."

"Yes."

He lowered his voice and pressed closer to her. "Look, Maureen, can't you give me another chance? Everyone makes mistakes."

If she trusted her intuition, she would have sworn he was sincere. But he'd disarmed her once, and that was sufficient.

"Isn't it enough that we're business partners and now neighbors? Your first instincts were correct. Ending our relationship was the right thing to do."

So then why did she want him to draw her into his arms again the way he had that night by the river? Maybe she'd spooked him by telling him all her problems. But while he'd listened, he'd made her feel so loved and accepted. She longed to have that feeling once more, and knowing it just wasn't possible hurt.

"I never ended our relationship. You did that."

"Oh, really? That's not how it felt to me." She crossed her arms over her chest, hating that he was making her relive the humiliation of that last night.

"Maureen, I can't keep apologizing—"

"I'm not asking you to be sorry. I'm just asking you to leave. No further explanations expected. You got to know the real me and that scared you off. Believe me, I understand."

With one hand on his shoulder, she *pushed* him out the door. She was tempted to throw the basket of muffins after him, but couldn't bring herself to commit that final act of rejection. Instead, she carried the baking to the kitchen, where she set the muffins on the counter next to the package of paper plates.

She'd convinced Jake to leave, and that was good. But now her house seemed colder and emptier than ever.

THE NEXT DAY JAKE WAS washing his truck in the driveway when he saw Holly step out tentatively onto the small porch landing of her new home. When she glanced at him, he waved, sending an arc of water flying in her direction from the saturated sponge he'd been using to scrub squished dragonflies from his headlights.

Holly sauntered over. She was in denim shorts and a pale pink T-shirt. Her feet were bare, her toenails each painted a different pastel color. He couldn't tell if she'd done the same thing with her fingernails. She had her hands behind her back.

"Why don't you just drive through a car wash?" she asked.

Which was probably what her mother usually did. "These bugs are pretty tenacious," he explained. "How do you like the new place?"

She shrugged and kicked at a pebble on the concrete parking pad. "It's okay, I guess. My new room is way bigger than my old one used to be. Thanks for taking down that wall."

"No problem."

"And thanks for the muffins, too. They were pretty tasty, even though they looked kind of weird. I brought back the container." From behind her back she pulled out the plain wicker basket with the napkin—no doubt freshly laundered—folded neatly in the center.

"You could've kept it, but that's okay. Put it by the door and I'll take it inside when I'm finished with this job."

"Okay." She did what he'd asked, then came back. "Do you have another sponge? I could work on the other headlight."

He thought. "Yeah. There's one in the laundry room. Hang on." He strode into the open garage and went in to the house via the side door. He couldn't find the sponge but brought out a rag she could use if she really did want to help.

He wasn't sure why she did. Weren't adolescents supposed to shirk chores at every opportunity?

"Here." He tossed her the remains of a once-favorite T-shirt.

"Thanks." She immersed it in the bucket of soapy water, then set to work. He watched her arm muscles flex and relax as she scrubbed. She was really putting some elbow grease into the effort.

"You and Mom don't see each other much anymore, do you?"

Jake moved from the headlight to the grill. "What do you mean?"

"Well, you haven't been around. You guys used to go out for dinner...."

"That's true," he conceded, wishing it still were. If only he'd appreciated what he'd had when he had it. Waiting to steal a glimpse of Maureen had become his new pastime. Not a very satisfying use of his leisure hours.

"So why'd you stop asking her out? Was it because of me?"

"What makes you think that?"

Holly put two hands on the rag and scrubbed even harder. "Well, you know, I kind of acted like a baby at first and got upset. But I'm used to the idea now and, well, almost kind of like it.... That is, I like *you*. You're okay."

Oh, no. Now he'd let down the kid as well as her mother. And he had no clue how to explain the situation to her. "I like you, too, Holly. And your mother."

"So maybe you'll ask her out again sometime."

She appeared so hopeful. "I'd like to. But I doubt she'll say yes."

"She might," Holly countered. "She's been listening to a lot of sad music lately, like she did right after Dad left for South America. I bet she could do with something to look forward to."

The idea of Maureen feeling blue caused a twinge of bitterness. All those stirred-up memories of Rod were probably getting her down. Probably she'd cared more for her husband than she'd ever let on.

"I'm not so sure dinner with me would be the solution," he finally said to Holly. After all, he'd made several overtures to Maureen already, and each time she'd shot him down. If Maureen gave him the slightest bit of encouragement he knew he'd try again. He hadn't given up completely. At least, not yet.

MAUREEN STOOD AT THE living room window, hoping she was far enough back that no one could see her. This past week she'd noticed Holly making excuses to spend time with Jake. Tuesday, she'd helped him wash his truck. Wednesday, she'd waited until the moment she saw him step out his front door to take her scooter for a run right past his house.

Jake had seemed fascinated with the contraption and had accepted Holly's offer to give it a try. Observing surreptitiously Maureen had laughed as he scrambled for balance the first few minutes. Soon, however, Jake got the hang of it, and he and Holly had taken turns rounding the curve of the cul de sac.

Today, Jake had come home the owner of a gleaming chrome scooter, with flashing lights on the rear wheel. Maureen had been sitting at her desk in her bedroom when she'd heard Holly's delighted whoop. Seconds later, the front door had opened and Holly called, "I'm going out with Jake, Mom. See you later."

Maureen had finished reading to the end of the paragraph, marked the contract, then gone downstairs to check out the window again.

Now as the two of them raced down the sidewalk, her amused smile slowly faded, replaced with a heavy ache in her chest.

She recognized the feeling from the countless times she'd seen her daughter and her husband having fun together. It was the pain of being the outsider, the unwanted one.

So go out and join them this time, an inner voice counseled. She was tempted. But how could she face Jake, especially in front of her daughter? He knew everything about her now. She had no safe mask to hide behind anymore.

CHAPTER TWELVE

SATURDAY MORNING MAUREEN was in the kitchen making breakfast when Cathleen called.

"Poppy's been a little dejected lately. I thought we'd cheer her up by having a big family dinner. Are you and Holly free?"

Maureen glanced at the calendar she'd hung by the phone. All those empty white boxes were depressing. "Yes, we can make it. What's wrong with Poppy?"

"Something to do with Harvey, I suspect, but Poppy just sighs whenever I bring up the subject. Maybe you could get Jake to worm something out of Harvey."

Maureen scraped the fruit she'd been cutting into a bowl. "If you want Jake's help, you'd better ask him yourself."

"I don't like the sound of that. What's going on, Maureen? I thought you two were dating...."

"We haven't seen each other in ages."

"Well, why not?" Cathleen asked, clearly exasperated. "You were off to such a great start."

"That's all it ended up to be. We played a bit of

tennis and went out for dinner a couple of times. But we just didn't click."

Cathleen became quiet for a moment, then repeated carefully, "You didn't *click?*"

"No." Maureen stared vacantly out the window, remembering...Jake teasing her when she missed a return in tennis, holding her by the river while she cried, making love to her against the door in his foyer....

No, they hadn't clicked. It'd been more like an explosion that had shattered them both when it was over. Well, shattered her, anyway. As far as she could tell, Jake was doing just fine.

"Well, I wish you'd told me," Cathleen said. "I wouldn't have invited him to dinner, then."

Oh, great. "So he's coming, too?"

"Not only coming. He's offered to drive you and Holly. He told me to pass on the message."

The weasel. He'd known she'd refuse if he asked her directly.

"Why do you suppose he agreed to come to dinner and volunteered—most eagerly, I might add— to drive you to the B and B?"

"I have no idea."

"Oh, really? If there's one thing I recognize, it's when a man is interested in a woman."

"Great." Maureen tossed the fruit peelings into the trash. "Why don't you go ahead and start printing up wedding invitations, then?"

"Click," Cathleen replied. *"Click, click, click."*
Maureen had no choice but to hang up on her.

EVEN WITH HOLLY IN THE back seat, chatting about
her plans for the rest of summer vacation, Maureen
felt uncomfortable sitting next to Jake as he drove.
She hadn't been this close to him in more than a
month. Efforts to focus on the road ahead were un-
successful. All she noticed were his large, steady
hands on the steering wheel, his broad shoulders taking up more than his share of the cab space, how
relaxed he appeared.

He seemed to be looking forward to the upcoming
evening. She dreaded every minute, aware that her
sisters would be poking and prodding her every
chance they got.

*Why don't you like him? What happened between
the two of you?*

At the B and B, Kip barreled out the door to welcome them, followed by Amanda and Billy. The little kids absolutely adored Holly—or "Howwy," as
Amanda called her. In the kitchen, Poppy had her
sleeves rolled high and her hair pinned up. She was
in her element.

"This is so wonderful to have everyone together!
Maureen, you can mash the potatoes. Dylan is carving the tenderloin and Cathleen and Kelly are tossing salads. Jake, maybe you could open the wine."

By giving everyone a job, she made them all feel

important and needed and part of the clan. Maureen observed this, somehow still feeling outside the magic circle.

Dinner was served at the table in the dining room. At first the talk was general, but Maureen wasn't surprised when her daughter worked the conversation around to the Beckett murder.

"Dylan, why did the police think at first that you'd done it?"

"Good question, Holly. Mostly because I hadn't made any secret of how much I despised my stepfather. I guess the police figured I was just trying to stir up trouble."

"The police in general," Maureen inquired, "or primarily Springer?" She'd run into the staff sergeant in town the other day and ended up having coffee with him. Their resulting half-hour conversation had been vaguely disquieting.

"I'd say Springer," Kelly said. "But I'm not sure we should be talking about this around the kids. Billy, sit still and then you can have some dessert."

"You'll like it," Poppy promised the young boy. "I made regular pies for the grown-ups but a special chocolate cream one for you and Amanda."

Billy stopped wiggling. Even Holly perked up. "Can I have some chocolate pie, too?"

"You bet. In fact, Holly, will you come to the kitchen and help me serve?"

Once dessert was finished, Holly took the little

kids to watch a video in the next room. Cathleen topped up everyone's coffee. When she came to Maureen's mug, Maureen demurred.

"No, thanks." She covered the top of her mug with her hand. Throughout the meal, she'd noticed how comfortable Jake seemed in his spot between Poppy and Amanda. He'd helped the little girl cut her meat, kept the wineglasses filled at all times and still followed the conversation with the ease of someone who'd been around the family for a long time.

Of course, he was Dylan's cousin, so in a way he really was part of this family.

For some reason, that knowledge bothered her. This was *her* family, damn it.

"Where's Harvey tonight?" Mick asked.

Like a drop of food coloring in a glass of water, quiet spread out from his remark. From the expression on Kelly's face, she was kicking her husband under the table. Poor guy, he remained clueless that what he'd said was wrong. Although he'd certainly picked up on the fact that he'd made a gaffe.

"I'm sorry…"

"It's okay, Mick." Poppy stirred her coffee and sighed. "You all deserve the truth. I've been putting off telling you because I myself didn't want to face it."

"If Harvey's seeing another woman, I'm going to run him over with my Jeep," Cathleen promised.

Poppy laughed weakly. "No. Not another woman. Actually, he asked me to marry him."

Maureen blinked. From Poppy's glum countenance, this was the last news she'd expected. "Why, that's wonderful!"

"Wonderful, yes." Poppy tapped her spoon against the tabletop. "Except he wants me to move back to the Maritimes with him."

"Oh, no," Kelly said softly.

"'No' is right. I told him I couldn't do it." Her gaze swept over all of them, and Maureen felt a tug on her heart, one she hadn't experienced in a long time, not since her mother had been alive.

"But if you love him..." Cathleen's voice wavered.

"I do. But love at seventy is different from love at your age. You and Dylan will be building a family together. That pursuit is long gone for Harvey and me."

"Still, you'd have each other," Maureen pointed out.

"Yes, and Harvey's a wonderful man. But five years ago if you'd asked for my greatest regret, I'd have told you it was that I had no grandchildren. Can you imagine how I felt when I discovered that in fact I had three?"

"What a shock," Maureen said.

"My emotions were so mixed. Happy, excited, curious...but sad, also. All the years I've missed...well, I don't want to miss any more. I want to be here for my great-grandchildren while they're young. For Holly, and Billy and Amanda. And all the little ones I know will come.''

Maureen's throat tightened. Did any of them really deserve this woman, who asked so little of them and was so grateful for any attention she received? When Maureen herself had been really hurting, Poppy was the one who'd noticed, who'd reached out with a loving heart and tried to help.

''Well, we've had no shortage of problems since you've met us, have we?'' Cathleen asked on a half laugh, half sob. ''No wonder you're afraid to move away. God, you must think we're a pathetic lot.''

''No.'' Poppy's voice was firm. She wiped tears from her eyes and sat up straight. ''You are wonderful girls. Your mother would be so proud of each of you.'' Her expression bespoke her fierce loyalty.

Kelly, who was sitting next to Poppy, reached over to give her a hug. ''Billy and Amanda love you to death. We all do.''

''And if you really do want to stay, then you must. This is your home for as long as you want it,'' Cathleen said.

''Oh, Cathleen, you little love. I've always realized I can't live here forever. When you and Dylan get the ranch back—and I know that you will, I feel it in my bones—you'll close down the B and B.''

''That's what we'd planned,'' Cathleen conceded.

"But it doesn't have to be that way. You're more than capable of running this place on your own. Face it, I've been a mere figurehead since the first day you moved in."

"And such a pretty figurehead," Dylan murmured. "But let me second that offer, Poppy. The lodge is your home. Period."

Poppy's pale, freckled skin colored. "You're being too generous."

"You're the one who always does too much for others," Kelly pointed out.

"Harvey's going to be annoyed with us," Maureen said. "For trying to bribe you into staying."

"You don't need to bribe me, love. Nothing could make me leave now that I know you all want me here."

SOMEHOW CATHLEEN AND MAUREEN ended up alone in the kitchen, washing things that wouldn't fit in the dishwasher.

"Cathleen, did you ever wonder why Springer was so eager to pin Jilly's murder on Dylan?"

Cathleen's eyes became guarded. "He thought he did it, I suppose. Why?"

"Just wondering." She squirted soap in the sink and turned on the faucet. "Kelly told me you dated Springer for a while when Dylan was gone."

"I dated a lot of guys."

"Ever think this particular fellow might still be

in love with you? That he might have personal reasons for wanting Dylan out of the picture?''

Cathleen regarded her for several long moments, then nodded. "Actually, Dylan thought the same thing. Last autumn, when Springer discovered the gun under Dylan's mattress, Dylan wondered if Springer had been the one to plant it there. But then we found out it was James Strongman, trying to pin the blame on his brother-in-law.''

"I just ask because I ran into the staff sergeant downtown. I barely know the man and my impression was the only reason he flagged me down was to ask about you. Which he did in some detail. Cathleen, he's not over you.''

"Well, he didn't show up at our wedding, even though he was invited, so you could be right.''

Maureen added more hot water, then started washing the crystal wineglasses. "By the way, that was a wonderful offer you and Dylan made to Poppy.''

"It's all assuming we eventually are able to move back to the ranch. But I'm pretty confident about that.''

"You're always confident," Maureen stated. "Even when things were at their blackest for you. When the police found the gun and Dylan was arrested and almost charged…you never lost your belief that everything would work out in the end.''

Cathleen dried the carving knife carefully and put it back in the knife rack. "And it did, right?"

"But truthfully…" Maureen levered herself up to the countertop. "Didn't you ever wonder if Dylan might actually be guilty?"

Cathleen shook her head, then shrugged. "Maybe for a split second. No longer than that."

"But how could you be so sure?"

"Because—" Cathleen cut off her own sentence. She put her hands on her hips and eyed her sister. "You don't have much faith in love, do you?"

The comment caught Maureen off guard. She slid from the countertop and moved to the table. "As someone I know once said, I'm a cynical old broad."

"I don't recall using those exact words." Jake was standing in the doorway that led from the dining room. Leaning against the wall, he had his index finger wound in the handle of a coffee mug.

"Close enough," Maureen replied. Suddenly she was short of breath. She wrapped her dish cloth around the handle of the fridge and tried to contrive an escape plan.

But Jake was moving closer, limiting her options. He had that light in his eyes, as if he was thinking of kissing her.

"Did anyone hear that?" Cathleen asked.

"What?" Jake asked, his gaze still on Maureen.

"I can't say for sure. Just this *clicking* sound."

She winked at her sister. "I'm out of here, folks. The two of you are stuck with the roasting pan."

"Thank God," Maureen called after her. "I'd rather wash *ten* roasting pans than put up with your prattle."

"What's got you all worked up?" Jake asked. He rested a hand on her shoulder as if that was the most natural thing in the world for him to do. To move away now would seem petty.

"Jake, you've never had sisters, so you wouldn't understand."

"You were talking about trust, I know that much. You were wondering how Cathleen could've trusted Dylan so much that she always believed in him."

"Yes. So?"

"Well, it's got me thinking that that's our problem, too. I hurt you and broke your trust. Now I need to earn it back again."

"That's one way to look at it," she agreed. "Or we could just count our losses and move on."

"But how would that get us any further ahead? Maureen, no matter who you end up with, eventually, at some point, he's going to let you down. The right person, though, will try to make up for it when he's made a mistake."

The right person. Was it really as simple as that? And if it was, how was a woman supposed to know when she'd found him?

CHAPTER THIRTEEN

THE NEXT MORNING, Holly came into Maureen's bathroom to borrow a comb.

"What's wrong with *your* comb?" Maureen was annoyed with her hair, the cowlick in front was totally out of control.

"Nothing, except I can't find it." Holly sorted through the wicker basket containing Maureen's makeup and pulled out a lipstick. She snapped off the lid and inspected the color. "Gross. It's like, *brown.*"

Maureen held out her hand. "That's cappuccino cream, *darling*. And it's the perfect color for a thirty-three-year-old woman on a hot summer day."

"Whatever." Holly recapped the tube and dropped it into her mother's palm. "Why are you going to all this fuss just to sit at your desk and work all day?"

"Since when is brushing my hair and putting on lipstick a fuss? I do these things every day. Especially now that we each have our own bathroom."

"Yeah. That is *one* good thing about this place," Holly conceded. She slid off the counter and went to the window, where she opened the blinds. "I wonder what Jake's doing this morning."

Maureen rubbed her lips together, smoothing out the cappuccino cream. She was beginning to suspect that this matchmaking stuff of her sisters had worn off on her daughter.

"I have no idea what Jake's doing."

"He still likes you, you know."

"Really?"

Suddenly Holly's posture shifted from loose and restless to tense and excited. She cranked open the window and pressed her nose flat against the screen. "Hey, Jake!"

Maureen ignored an impulse to move so that she, too, could see out the window. Instead, she picked up a small bottle of perfume and sprayed behind her ears.

Jake called back a reply, his words too muffled for Maureen to discern their meaning. Holly had no trouble, though.

"Great! I'll get my scooter and be right down!" Before passing through the bathroom door, she paused to tell her mother, "You know, those scooters are a lot of fun. You should get one, too."

The suggestion was enough to freeze Maureen to the spot for several seconds. If she was ever going to stop being the outsider with her daughter, she had to start somewhere. Maybe this was just the place.

MAUREEN LOCATED A SCOOTER at the hardware store, but by the time she drove back home, Jake and Holly were no longer on the street. She found them on the deck at the back of Jake's town house. They'd abandoned their scooters—now propped up against the side wall—for the lure of soft drinks and home-barbecued burgers.

Jake was at the grill and Holly was prone on a wooden bench that ran along the railing of the deck.

"You're back," he said.

"That smells good." She went to the cedar table, where all the fixings had been unceremoniously laid out. Cheese slices still in plastic wrap, catsup in a squeeze bottle, mustard with a knife in the jar.

"I have an extra patty on the grill if you're tempted."

Jake's smile promised more than lunch. Maureen glanced in her daughter's direction, but Holly appeared to have fallen asleep in the hot midday sun. She hadn't said a word, or even moved, since Maureen's arrival.

"I'll say yes to the burger," Maureen replied carefully. "What's with Holly? Did you wear her out on the scooter?"

"Apparently so, although you wouldn't have known it half an hour ago. Do you mind passing me those tongs from the table?"

Later Maureen realized he'd merely invented an

excuse to get her closer. As soon as she was within arm's reach, he captured her hand.

"I enjoyed dinner last night. You've got a great family." The intensity of his expression bore no relation to his words.

"They have their moments."

Gently, he drew her nearer. Then bent his head and grazed her ear with his mouth. She felt the heat of his breath in a tingle that traveled all the way to her toes.

"I wanted to kiss you good-night, but as soon as I stopped the truck, you dashed for your door."

"Holly was there. Besides, we weren't exactly on a date."

"But you wanted the kiss anyway, didn't you? Just like you'd kind of like one now." He hooked his arm around her waist and pulled her hard against his hip.

Maureen hated to admit he was right. Especially with Holly on the bench just a couple of meters away. She put a hand to his chest.

"Jake, the burgers are burning."

"They are *not* burning, Mother. You're the one who always says you have to make sure to cook ground beef all the way through to kill the bacteria."

So. Holly had *not* been sleeping. Maureen stepped back from Jake and told herself that having been caught almost kissing a man by her daughter was not a big deal.

"You're right," she said. "Let me check to see if there's any pink."

"Mom always inspects our burgers, even the ones at the fast-food joints."

"*Especially* the ones at the fast-food places," Maureen said in a voice that was still a little too highly pitched.

Obligingly, Jake flipped one of the fatter patties onto a plastic plate and handed her a knife. She made a slit at the center and checked carefully.

"Looks perfect."

"Lunch is served, then." Jake added the rest of the patties to the plate and turned off the gas to the barbecue. "Load up, everyone."

The burgers were even more delicious than they appeared.

"What do you put in them?" Maureen asked.

"Lots of garlic, Parmesan and lemon juice."

"Really? They're fabulous."

Maureen had to admit her feelings where Jake was concerned were softening. He seemed to genuinely want her company. That had to mean she hadn't completely turned him off. Keep things casual and light; that was the key. A date here or there, a kiss, even making love did not have to signify a lifelong commitment. With the right attitude she could handle Jake.

When they were finished eating and Maureen

tried to stack the lunch dishes to carry inside, Jake stopped her.

"I'll put the leftovers in the kitchen so we don't get any unwanted visitors, but we can leave the dishes until later." He glanced at Holly. "Up for another scooter race?"

"You bet!" Holly straddled the cedar bench, then hopped down to the lawn. "Coming, Mom?"

Jake had whisked the food indoors and was already back on the deck. Still, the picnic table was a mess and Maureen really hated to leave dirty dishes unattended. She could clean them up while Jake and Holly... But, no. That was a trap she'd fallen into too many times in the past.

She set down the stack of dishes and smiled at her daughter. "Want to see what I have in my trunk?"

"No! You didn't!"

When Maureen nodded, Holly whooped. "Mom bought a scooter!"

"You'll have to teach me how to use it," Maureen cautioned.

"No problem. They're easy. Come on, Jake."

Casually, Jake slung his arm around Maureen's waist. "You bet. This is one sight I don't want to miss. Should I get the video camera?"

"That depends. Do you mind getting blood splattered on it?"

Her concerns about catching on to the scooter

proved unfounded. Riding it was actually simple. Soon she was joining in Jake and Holly's races, and even managed to win one. Holly emerged triumphantly as the overall champ, however.

Later, they went out for dessert. On the way home Jake stopped so Maureen could rent a movie she'd been eager to see, a historical epic that lost Holly's interest about a quarter of the way through.

"I'm going to my room to listen to some music," she said, taking the half-finished bowl of popcorn with her.

Frankly, Jake wasn't sorry to see her go. The evening had been pleasant, but with Holly around, he felt he had to keep his distance from Maureen. Now he shuffled over on the couch to be next to her. When she raised her eyebrows as if challenging his nerve, he reached for her slightly sticky hand and raised it to his mouth.

First he kissed the back of her hand, then opened his mouth to taste the tip of her finger. "Mmm, salty and buttery, just like popcorn."

Maureen pushed back on the sofa in an attempt to stand.

"Where are you going?"

"To wash my hands."

He blocked her with his shoulders. "I'll be glad to do that for you." Deliberately, he placed her second finger in his mouth. Maureen swallowed.

"You're not watching the film," she pointed out.

"So what?" He didn't care how many Academy Awards the picture had won. The woman beside him was much more intriguing. That she might allow him a second chance was an opportunity he didn't intend to blow.

"Maureen? Let's forget about the movie and talk."

She shifted her head to see past him to the screen. "But this is the best part...."

He turned her face toward his. "It's on video. You can watch it tomorrow."

"There'll be a late fee...."

He dug into his pants pocket and located a few dollar coins. "This should cover it."

Maureen rolled her eyes. "What do you want to talk about?"

"Us."

"I can't believe it. Men *never* want to talk about relationships."

"Well, I do."

Maureen, who'd insisted on being in control of the remote, finally clicked the power to the TV off. "Fine, then. Let's talk."

She folded her arms over her chest and leveled her gaze at him. Once more he was reminded that she was a lawyer. In a boardroom somewhere, she'd probably given this same look to an opposing attorney, letting him know that she was done bargaining.

Well, he wasn't interested in bargains anymore,

either. He was a man who'd fallen in love, a little too quickly, a little too hard. The ground had come at him fast and he'd done his best to soften the landing. And hurt Maureen in the process.

"It's embarrassing for a thirty-eight-year-old man to admit he acted like a scared kid," he began. "But that's what I did, and all I can say now is I'm sorry."

He wanted to go further. To tell her he loved her. For the first time in his life the words *I love you* beat in his chest like a caged bird that was eager to be free.

But Maureen interrupted him. "Maybe your instinct to pull away was right. Relationships are tricky under the best circumstances. Why choose a woman with a kid and a lot of messy baggage left over from her first marriage?"

"Because I can't get her out of my mind?"

Maureen blinked but said nothing. Had he stunned her into silence?

"I've done a lot of thinking these past few weeks. The way I see it, there are three reasons we belong together. Number one, I love you. Number two, I—"

She pushed her hand against his chest. "What do you mean, you love me?" The words came out fast and incredulous, sort of like a chocoholic asking his roommate, *What do you mean you ate the last slice of chocolate cake?*

"Is it a crime?"

"You hardly know me. It's only been a few months. You can't love me already."

He placed his hand over her mouth. "Wait. I was speaking and I wasn't finished. Now, then. Number two, I'm very fond of Holly, and I think she likes me, too."

Even as he cautiously removed his hand, Maureen's lips stayed pressed together. Good. She couldn't argue against that one.

"Number three, your sisters approve of me. That's got to count for something."

Finally, a hint of a smile turned up one corner of Maureen's mouth. "You seem to have all the bases covered."

"Except home base." He took both of her hands, knowing his situation was as precarious as ever. He'd told her how he felt about her. But how did she feel about him?

It was a question he didn't dare ask. But maybe a kiss would tell him all he needed to know. He'd been wanting to kiss her for so long now. With any luck, Holly wouldn't interrupt this time. He lowered his head.

Maureen's lips tasted like her hands. Salty, with a hint of butter flavor. Her mouth was warm and inviting, and yet he sensed a hesitation that reminded him that she was far more sensitive than she allowed most people to realize.

He let his hands cup her head, sinking his fingers into the thick strands of her hair, tilting her face so that he could approach this a little more thoroughly.

Predictably, the kiss only made him want to love her more thoroughly, but he kept his hands away from the temptation of her breasts beneath her cotton T-shirt and the curvy line of her hips and bottom in her faded jeans.

Instinct warned him to go slow, even when Maureen's soft moan told him she was in the same state of delirium as he was. They snuggled back into the sofa, with Maureen curled under his right arm. He pulled her legs over his thighs, to rest along the length of the cushions, but that was as daring as he got.

He kept his lovemaking to kisses and caresses of her face and her hair. Eventually, however, there came a point where he really couldn't take it anymore.

"Maureen, I want you so bad I've got to go home."

She laughed. "I know what you mean."

In that moment it was tempting to ask her if she would consider…

But she was leading him by the hand to the front door. "It's really important that we take this one step at a time," she said. "I've done some thinking, too. Rushing into bed was our big mistake. We weren't emotionally ready for that step."

He hated to admit that she might be right, but of course she was. That he was emotionally ready *now* didn't matter. There were mistakes from the past to make up for.

"I'll see you in the morning?" he asked at the door. He ran a hand down the side of her head, cupping her face for a moment before relinquishing his hold.

"So soon?"

"Yes," he insisted. "I have some fresh blueberries. We'll have pancakes."

"And Holly?"

"Tell her to bring her scooter. I demand a rematch."

CHAPTER FOURTEEN

MAUREEN LAY IN HER COOL, still bed, listening to the creek and thinking of Jake. Tonight he'd said he loved her. He'd kissed her as though he meant it, then invited her over for breakfast as though he couldn't wait to see her again.

What was happening here? This wasn't the casual relationship she'd schooled herself to expect from him. But perhaps Jake was one of those people who said *I love you* easily. Perhaps he truly did want to use up the blueberries in his fridge before they went bad.

Her thoughts were so focused on Jake she expected to dream about him all night. Yet at two in the morning when she woke in a state of panic, it was Conrad Beckett and his wife, Linda, she was thinking of.

Why hadn't she gone to visit Linda before she'd left Calgary? Or at least called? In her dream, Linda had been trapped inside that garage with Conrad, crying out for someone to help her.

When dawn lightened the noose of night, Maureen bundled up in her housecoat and took a cup of warmed milk, flavored with coffee, out on her deck. It was so cold she needed a blanket, too. After wrapping herself snugly, she watched the colors of the world slowly come into focus. The one thing she knew was that the sun could not set again without her getting in touch with Linda.

She must have dozed for a while out there on her deck. When she opened her eyes, daylight was well established. According to her wristwatch, it was eight o'clock. Jake would soon be flipping pancakes. If she didn't want her cowlick to be flipping, too, she'd better take a shower.

Fifteen minutes under hot pulsing water made her feel like a new woman. Wearing her robe with a towel wrapped turban-style around her hair, she tapped on Holly's door.

"Want to come to Jake's for breakfast? Blueberry pancakes..."

"Oh, Mo-o-om." Holly rolled over. "Can't I sleep a little longer?"

"Fine with me. There's cereal in the cupboard when you get hungry."

"Cereal?" She groaned. "Okay, I'll be ready in fifteen minutes."

Maureen used the time to dress, put on makeup, do her hair. Then she and Holly walked the short distance to Jake's town house. When Maureen knocked, the door fell open.

"Come through to the kitchen," Jake called.

He was at the counter, measuring coffee, wearing a blue T-shirt with the Grizzly Peaks logo in bright white relief. In his ubiquitous Dutch oven now sputtered at least a dozen sausages. "Those are great. Chicken and apple. You'll love 'em," he promised Holly.

A hot grill stood at the ready on the counter by the sink.

"Could you throw a gob of pancake batter on that?" Jake asked her.

"Sure. A *gob* it is." She filled the large spoon sitting in the bowl and then let the creamy, blueberry-studded liquid stream down in a perfect circle.

With the coffee going, Jake turned to Holly. "How about a glass of juice? Or would milk be better?"

"Juice," Holly said. "Thanks."

"Maybe I should cut up some grapefruit, as well. Want to help?"

As she watched Jake's ease in the kitchen and with Holly, it wasn't difficult to picture him as a father. The moment the thought crossed her mind, though, Maureen frowned. She reminded herself she wanted to keep her relationship with Jake casual. Yet her responses to him were anything but. She flipped the batch of pancakes onto a plate.

"Who's first?"

When they were all sitting around the table, Maureen broached the topic that had been on her mind since waking.

"I had a dream about Linda Beckett last night."

"Oh?" Jake looked up from pouring syrup.

"I meant to visit her before we moved. But I was busy and I kept putting it off." What did you say to a woman whose daughter had been murdered and whose husband subsequently took his own life? Now she felt ashamed that she'd taken the easy way out.

"It's still not too late."

There he went again. Reading her mind. "Could I call her from here?"

"Sure. The phone's right behind you."

"Are you going to visit her, Mom?"

Maureen was dialing information for the number. A recorded voice asked, *What city, please?* "Calgary," she said, then covered the mouthpiece. "If she invites me, yes."

"Can I come along? I've always wanted to see the inside of their house."

Maureen studied her daughter's expression uneasily. She didn't want Holly's interest in this case to become a preoccupation. It couldn't be mentally healthy.

What number, please?

"Linda or Conrad Beckett on Sydenham Road."

Hold for that number, please.

"We could make the trip together," Jake suggested. "I have some more supplies for the lodge to pick up."

"Good idea, Jake!"

Holly's enthusiasm wasn't something Maureen wanted to squelch. She listened as the number she'd been waiting for was repeated, then she hung up and dialed Linda Beckett. It was nine-thirty now, hopefully not too early to call.

Jake and Holly started clearing the table. Linda picked up on the third ring. She sounded glad to hear from Maureen and quickly invited her to drop by any time that day.

"I'm glad I phoned," Maureen said after she'd hung up. "She seemed genuinely happy that I wanted to visit. And she extended an invitation to you, too, Holly."

"How about we leave as soon as we finish these dishes?"

Maureen was amazed, and pleased, when Holly ran a sinkful of water and began washing the grill, then the Dutch oven. Maureen and Jake loaded the dishwasher and wiped down the counters.

"Let's take my car," Jake suggested.

"Can I change my shoes first?" Holly asked.

Jake and Maureen were waiting in the driveway when Holly came running back ten minutes later. She was wearing her new platform shoes, black with two-and-a-half-inch soles. A strong wind might unbalance the slender girl, but her shoes would keep her firmly planted on the ground.

On closer examination, Maureen noticed colored lip gloss, eye shadow and blush on her daughter's face. Since Holly had been fairly subtle, she decided not to object.

Holly ensconced herself in the back seat with her portable CD player and headphones. Maureen climbed into the passenger captain seat in the front and slipped her travel mug into the cup holder next to Jake's.

"Ready?" he asked.

She nodded, ignoring the surging anxiety in her stomach. She was glad they were going to visit Linda, knew it was the right thing, but still she was apprehensive. How would Linda react when she saw them? Perhaps allowing Holly to come along had been a mistake. If the conversation got heavy, she might not be able to handle it.

"You're not looking forward to this," Jake stated.

"Not at all. Isn't that awful?"

"Maybe natural. Knowing what to say to people who've lost so much is hard. You, having an only daughter like the Becketts, probably understand more than most what they've gone through. That makes it even harder."

It was true. How often had she thought, *If that had happened to Holly, I would want to die.* It wasn't that you loved a child more when she was the only one you had. At least Maureen didn't think you did. But somehow only children seemed more vulnerable.

"Rod wanted just one child." Now, why had she volunteered that? "Would you like to have kids of your own, Jake?"

"Haven't given the matter much thought." He pushed his sunglasses down his nose a notch, so she could see his eyes. "Until recently."

Maureen deliberately turned back to gaze out the front windshield, but her heart was beating so quickly she was afraid the buttons on her jacket might start to clatter.

Did Jake mean their abbreviated discussion about birth control had sent his thoughts in that direction? Or was he referring to his feelings about her and their relationship? That it might be the latter was terrifying. But also exciting. More children...it was a dream she'd relinquished long ago. If only Rod...

Old pain. Familiar pain. Maureen didn't want to have to deal with it. Not when she would soon be seeing Linda. So she focused on the scenery, instead. They were in the foothills now, prime Alberta ranch land. Maureen spotted a herd of cattle and noticed how much the springtime calves had grown already.

Calves. Babies. Seemed her mind was set to play the same track over and over today.

"That was quite a sigh," Jake said. "Heavy thoughts?"

She hadn't realized she'd made a sound. "I guess so. Every now and then I look at Holly and can't believe she was once the baby I held in my arms. You saw her this morning, in those shoes and that makeup. Soon she'll be off to college and moving out...."

"Hey, not that soon." Jake laughed. "She's only *twelve.*"

Maureen didn't argue. She wasn't sure she could explain. Maybe it wasn't the idea of Holly growing up that was so painful, but the memory of all the years they'd lost. Years when she'd spent far more time with her clients than with her own daughter.

They passed the signs welcoming them to Calgary, one in English, then another in French, erected the year Calgary had hosted the Winter Olympics. Soon Jake veered off the highway and onto Sarcee Trail.

In the back, Holly emerged from beneath her headphones to ask, "Are we there?"

"Almost," Jake replied. He turned onto Seventeenth Avenue and within minutes they'd arrived in their old neighborhood. Maureen considered asking Jake to drive by their former home, then decided against it, worried it might upset Holly. Instead, she directed him to the Becketts' mansion—there was no other word to describe the gorgeous Tudor home.

The first detail she noticed was the closed doors to the triple garage. In a flash of panic, she checked for any sign of exhaust fumes streaming from under the doors...then chided herself for an overactive imagination.

She was slow to get out of the truck. "Thanks for the ride, Jake."

"I'll make sure Linda's home before I drive off." He eased out from his seat, stretched his arms and shoulders, then followed Maureen and Holly up the beautiful flagstone walkway.

The large oak door was ajar. Maureen gave a tap. "Hello?"

Almost immediately, Linda was there. Her hair was pulled back from her face, and without makeup, her skin tone was uneven and her lips and eyes undefined. But she'd put on pearls and a silk top; her elegant loafers were Kenneth Cole.

"Maureen. It's nice of you to come by. And Holly. I haven't seen you since you were a baby." Linda stepped back, beckoning them inside. Maureen paused for a quick word with Jake.

"I'll pick you up in an hour?" he asked her.

"Thanks. That would be great."

"Is someone else with you?" Linda stepped onto the landing. The daylight, even with some of the sun's intensity muted by low cloud cover, seemed to cause her an almost physical pain. She held up one thin arm to shield her face.

"I'm Jake Hartman, Mrs. Beckett. I was just dropping the ladies off before I—"

"That name is familiar. Were you at the ranch that night? I'm sure I remember your name."

Linda had to be referring to the night Jilly was shot. Jake had reached the same conclusion.

"Yes. I was."

"You must come in, too," Linda said. Ignoring Jake's reluctance, she placed a hand lightly on his upper arm. "Please. I'd really appreciate it."

"If you're sure."

Linda was. She ushered him through the doorway, then shut and bolted the door.

"We'll take our drinks out on the patio," she said, leading them down the central hall, still clasping Jake's arm.

Maureen followed with Holly. Their footsteps echoed loudly on gleaming wood floors. Holly swiveled her head as she tried to take in all the beautiful features of the spacious home.

"It's so quiet, isn't it?" she whispered to her mother. "And impressive. I feel like I'm visiting a museum after hours."

That was it exactly, Maureen concurred silently. Linda led them past a dining room where twenty could have sat in comfort, to a more casual sunroom with French doors opening onto a patio.

Once outdoors, Maureen filled her lungs with fresh air, only then realizing that she'd been breathing shallowly while in the house. The view out there was refreshing. Perennial borders bloomed in golds and blues and pinks, and the freshly mown lawns would have made perfect golfing greens.

There were comfortable cushioned chairs to sit in, and a pitcher of lemonade and glasses stood on a nearby table. "My sister set me up for the afternoon," Linda explained, pointing to a stack of books and magazines, as well as a tray of fruit, crackers and cheese. "She's been living with me since Conrad died. She's at work right now."

"You and your sister must be very close," Maureen noted, recalling how the two of them had been inseparable at Linda's funeral.

"Lucky for me. Diane has really seen me through these past few months."

"I'm so sorry about Conrad," Maureen said.

"Yes. It's been very hard," Linda acknowledged honestly. Her hands trembled like an old lady's as she filled the glasses with lemonade. "In some ways, almost worse than when Jilly..." She paused, lines knotting her forehead.

"Jilly used to be my baby-sitter," Holly said.

Linda smiled. "That's right, dear. I'd forgotten. I remember when Jilly started that business. Conrad took her to the office so she could run off copies of her brochure. She was always so keen when she had a new idea. Nothing, no one, could stand in her way...."

Her pale eyes stared off into the trees along the far side of the property. Maureen, Jake and Holly were all silent out of respect for her memories. Then suddenly, Linda turned to Maureen.

"I was very glad you called this morning. As soon as I heard your voice, I knew that you were just the right person."

"For what?" Maureen felt a twinge of trepidation.

Linda pulled something out from beneath the pile of magazines. It was a white business-size envelope with Linda's name printed in bold black letters on the front.

"Conrad left this for me. But I haven't had the courage to read it." She passed it to Maureen.

The envelope was sealed. Maureen shot a look at Jake. His gaze on hers seemed to warn her to be careful. She nodded slowly, then glanced back at Linda.

"Open it," the older woman said. "I want you to read it."

Maureen didn't point out the obvious. That it was meant for Linda. "Maybe your sister—"

"No." Linda shook her head. "When you called this morning, I realized it had to be you. You knew Conrad and Jilly, but whatever's in that letter won't break you."

The way Linda expected it to break *her*.

"Are you sure, Linda?"

She nodded.

Maureen turned the envelope over in her hands several times. Slowly she filled her lungs with air, then slit the envelope open at the top. Inside was one folded piece of paper.

"Read it to me." Linda covered her face with her hands and waited.

Jake put a hand on Maureen's shoulder. *You can do it,* he seemed to be saying.

"'My dear Linda.'" In her mind, Maureen converted the voice to Conrad's. "'You always suspected there was more to that night than I ever told you. And you were right.'" She paused, aware of her daughter's nervous tension, and thankful for Jake's quiet support.

"Are you sure this is the way you want to hear this, Linda?"

"Please."

There was such anguish in that quietly spoken word. Maureen turned her eyes back to the handwritten page. "'I saw the gun, Linda. A woman was standing in the house at the window. The dining room window. She removed the screen, then took the gun in both hands. I didn't feel scared. I remember thinking at the time, *Now, what the hell is Rose Strongman doing with that gun?*'"

Rose Strongman! Dylan's mother. Maureen's hands started to shake. She felt Jake's fingers tighten on the clenched muscles along the top of her back. Voice trembling now, too, she continued.

"'I was so foolish, Linda. The firecracker went off at just that moment. Jilly screamed and I hugged her to me. Can you believe my stupidity? At just the moment that Rose was pulling the trigger of her gun, I pulled my daughter in front of me. And she died. But it should've been me.'"

Maureen stopped reading. "There's nothing else." She dropped the letter to the table, the dead man's words still ringing in her imagination. *It should've been me.*

Hands still covering her face, Linda didn't move. Maureen pushed back on her chair and went to her. Wrapping her arms around Linda's shoulders, she felt the woman's desperate vulnerability and could think of nothing to say.

Minutes ticked on. Eventually sounds began to penetrate the shocked, insulating silence. Traffic from the street, a few birds, the shuffling of Holly's feet as she swung them over the concrete paving stones.

"He's right," Linda said. "I knew he was holding something back. But I never pressed him to talk. What would the truth have changed? But maybe he would have found some relief..."

Maureen patted Linda's fine-boned, freckled hand. It felt very cold and fragile. The suffering she saw etched over every inch of the woman's face seemed beyond human endurance.

"The letter..." Jake cleared his throat and tried again. "We should let the police take a look at that letter."

"Of course," Linda said quietly. "Could you call them for me?"

CHAPTER FIFTEEN

JAKE LEFT TO FIND A PHONE. Maureen glanced back at the note. It had curled on the table like an infant in the fetal position. Linda picked it up, refolded it and returned it to the envelope.

"All of a sudden, I feel so tired."

"If you want to take a nap, we could wait in the truck." Maureen wasn't going to drive off and leave the woman to face the police alone.

"No, no. Make yourself at home." She shifted her chair to a reclining position, then turned suddenly to Holly. "Do you remember Jilly at all?"

"Yes. We used to pretend we were detectives. She taught me how to make a periscope."

Linda's lips inched up at the corners. "Why don't you go up to her room. She had a collection of china horses. Take one to remember her by. As a favor to me."

Holly eyed her mother. Maureen nodded. "Go ahead. I'll be right there."

After her daughter had disappeared inside, she stroked one of Linda's hands. "Are you sure you're okay? Can I get you anything?"

"I wish there was something that would help, Maureen."

They both knew there wasn't.

"Sometimes I envy Conrad," she continued. "I think how wonderful it would be if the pain could be gone. Even for five minutes. If I could just forget for five precious minutes…"

Imagining what it would feel like to be in this woman's skin, Maureen felt as if her own heart might collapse. "You're very brave," she told her.

"Not brave at all. Just a mother. I can't bear to die, because if I do, the biggest piece of what's left of my daughter will be gone, too."

MAUREEN STOPPED BRIEFLY in the kitchen, where Jake was speaking on a cordless phone. She placed a hand on his shoulder and pointed out toward the patio.

"Keep an eye on her," she mouthed. Despite her courageous words, Linda Beckett shouldn't be left alone. Especially right now, so soon after hearing the contents of that letter.

Jake covered the mouthpiece. "You okay?"

She nodded. But halfway up the stairs she realized she wasn't. Sharp pains started in her abdomen, then rose to her chest. She saw an open door down the hall and heard Holly moving around. She made it inside the room, then sank into a chair by the door, holding her gaze to the fresh vacuum tracks on the plush carpet as Holly explored.

Breathe in, breathe out. The spasms in her stomach were terrible. The ache in her heart just as bad. Life was so unfair, so unjust. Maureen wanted to cry for Linda's losses, but her own guilt choked back the tears. She still had *her* daughter. But did she deserve her?

Maureen focused on the room, which was beautifully decorated and immaculately clean, and realized instantly that she was visiting a shrine. *Linda sits here. In this very chair, hour after hour.* Maureen couldn't say how she knew this. She just did. Slowly she shifted her eyes from the neatly made bed to the bathrobe still hanging on a hook behind the door. Cosmetics were scattered on a vanity desk. One solitary white sock peeked out from the duster around the bed.

Each detail she noticed caused fresh jolts of pain.

The evidence of Jilly's love of horses was everywhere. From posters tacked over the expensive wallpaper, to nonfiction titles on equestrian topics in the bookshelves, as well as the china horse collection Linda had referred to.

Holly sat on a carved wooden rocking horse. It was so small her knees touched her chest. "This is cute." She dismounted, then went to the grouping of horses and fingered each one lightly. "Which one looks most like Cascade, do you think?"

Maureen forced herself to stand, to move toward her daughter. Searching, she spotted a smaller-size model, one with strong hindquarters. "This one could be a quarter horse."

Holly nodded, but she didn't pick it up. Instead she went to the bookshelf and began sorting through the volumes.

Maureen watched her, trying to imagine the thoughts that must play through Linda's mind day after day. How unfair that all these inanimate objects—a quilt, a tube of lipstick, a stupid glossy poster—could exist longer than the little girl who'd collected them.

We are all so fragile. At any second the one person we hold most dear can be stolen away from us. How did anyone who understood the truth of this find the strength to carry on living?

What if she were to lose Holly?

Maureen swallowed. Linda's suffering pervaded this room. Like cheap cologne it stuck to every nook and cranny, insistent, overpowering, sickening in its intensity. She had to leave...but Holly hadn't picked out her horse yet.

Her daughter was back at the china figurines now, trailing a hand over their glossy coats. Maureen was struck by how fragile she was. And was filled with an overpowering urge to tell her something she hadn't said in an awfully long time.

"Holly?"

"Yeah?"

Maureen's throat turned dry. She was afraid. What if Holly ignored her? Or worse, sneered?

"I don't tell you often enough that I love you, do I?"

Holly stayed crouched in front of the book-shelves. Maureen walked over the smoothly vacuumed carpet, until she could lay a hand on her daughter's shoulder. She was distressed to feel how Holly's muscles tightened with the contact. "I *do* love you, Holly. So very much..."

Holly spoke to the bookshelves. "I can't remember you ever saying that before. N-not even when you told me what happened to Dad."

Maureen knew she wasn't having a heart attack, but it almost felt like it. The pain in her stomach traveled upward, circled her heart and tried to crush it.

Why hadn't she told Holly she loved her that night? It had been such a terrible, terrible time. But she'd been so focused on Holly's loss she'd never thought to offer reassurance about what she still had.

It was, Maureen decided, a pretty pathetic excuse.

"I used to tell you I loved you every night when I tucked you in." When had she stopped? She couldn't remember, just as she didn't know when the last time was she'd held Holly's hand to cross the street, helped her with her shoelaces or buttoned her coat....

"You used to call me Mama. You'd hug me tight and refuse to let me go." *Stay and cuddle. Sing me another lullaby.*

Maureen scanned the framed photographs on the top shelf, above her daughter's head. Pictures of Jilly with her dad, another with her mom. One of the three of them in front of a Christmas tree.

She wondered if, after the shooting, Linda had been able to remember the last time she'd told Jilly she loved her. Probably she had. That must've been a comfort.

"Do you remember the last time *your* mother told you?"

"I'm not sure." Maureen cocked her head, bringing back the past. "I don't think she said the words often, but I always knew my mother loved me." She put her other hand on Holly. "Even though I never said the words, you knew, too, right?"

To hear a terrible sob burst from her daughter's mouth was the most painful shock.

"Oh, Holly!" Maureen dropped to her knees and engulfed her daughter in a hug as if she were an infant. Her lips pressed to the top of her daughter's head, she rocked Holly.

"Mommy…"

"My poor child." Maureen felt the vibrations from her crying right down to her bones. "I love you so much. So very, very much."

JAKE DIDN'T KNOW WHY Maureen and Holly were so quiet on the drive home. The day had been traumatic. Maybe they were just stressed. After handing over the letter, Linda had given a statement to the Calgary police, who'd then wanted to speak to each of them, as well. That had taken until almost four in the afternoon, at which point Maureen had suggested waiting until Linda's sister returned from work before leaving the older woman alone.

Before departing the city, they'd gone a bit out of their way to visit Peter's Drive-In, renowned for its hamburgers and shakes. He'd thought the food would revive them all, but apparently not even a root beer shake was going to lift anyone's spirits today.

Beside him, Maureen, still gazed out the window, but he was certain she was oblivious to the passing landscape. In the back, Holly's earphones had fallen to her neck. She was asleep, her mouth half-open, her head resting against the passenger window.

The temptation was great—he reached over to touch Maureen's hand. The contact was something he'd been craving for hours now. Seeing Linda Beckett all alone in that luxurious showcase home of hers had been a bit like visiting the Ghost of Christmas Future. Sure, Linda had lost her family because of tragedy, but if Jake never had a family, simply because he'd been too scared to make it happen, the end result wouldn't be much different.

One person, one house. Echoing hallways and solitary table settings. Most lonely of all, one person in bed by himself, waking every morning to nothing more human than a reflection in the bathroom mirror.

That was how Jake had lived ever since he'd left home. At first he'd savored his independence, but over the years, the pleasure had worn thin. Every time the solitude got to him, however, he'd just run out to the mountains with some friends. Hiking, skiing, climbing, biking—all were passions with him.

But at the end of the day, he still had to go home. Wouldn't it be nice if someone he loved, who loved him back, were there to share those hours?

Not *someone,* he corrected himself. Maureen. And Holly. And who knows—maybe another child or two in the future.

Whoa! He was getting ahead of himself. Maureen had turned her hand over and curled her fingers into his palm. That didn't mean he'd regained her trust. He'd barely managed to convince her that it was okay for them to spend more time together. How was he going to persuade her that they belonged under one roof, not three doors down from each other?

"I can't believe Rose Strongman shot that gun." The words burst out of Maureen as if she'd been trying to contain them but no longer could.

"It does seem far-fetched," Jake agreed. Yet if it

was true, what a tidy resolution to the case. Rose was dead; there would be no arrest, no trial, no messy complications.

Nevertheless, he didn't think Dylan would find much satisfaction in having the murder solved at the expense of his mother's reputation.

"It couldn't be Rose," Maureen insisted. "I remember Cathleen telling me that the reason Dylan ran off before their first wedding was that his mother told him she thought he'd shot Jilly."

A surmise Rose would never have made if *she'd* been the one to pull the trigger.

"You think Conrad was mistaken?"

"It's possible. It was almost dark and he had to be standing some distance from the window."

"But the letter didn't really leave room for any mistakes."

"Yes, he *did* sound certain. Oh, Jake, none of this makes any sense. I almost wish we hadn't gone to Linda's. Maybe she never would've opened that blasted letter...."

He realized she didn't mean what she was saying. The truth had to be faced, eventually, by all of them. But, like Maureen, he wasn't convinced they'd discovered it yet.

Somewhere out there, at least one more piece of the puzzle remained to be found.

WHEN HOLLY AWOKE the next morning, she knew right away something was different. She didn't have that sick, aching feeling in her chest.

For reassurance, she glanced at the framed photo of her dad, sitting next to her alarm clock on the nightstand. "Is that okay?" she asked him. "I still miss you, Daddy. I always will."

She sat up. Outside, she saw blue sky, fluffy clouds, familiar mountains.

Down the hall she could hear the radio station her mom listened to when she was working. It was after ten. She'd probably been at her desk for hours.

Holly climbed out of bed and dressed quickly. For some reason she felt shy about seeing her mother this morning, so she was glad she'd slept in. This way she could eat her toast alone at the kitchen table. After, she had work to do.

She grabbed her notebook and pen from under her bed, then tiptoed to the hall. The door to her mother's room was open and she was sitting at her desk, back to the hall, facing out the window.

"'Morning, Holly."

How had her mother known she was there?

"'Morning."

"Sleep okay?"

"Fine." Holly fingered the wooden ball on the top of the stair railing. "You?"

"Oh, good, thank you. What do you have planned today?"

"I thought I might go downtown for a few hours. Meet some friends. Is that all right?"

"I guess so." Her mother tapped a pen on her knee. "How about I meet you at the Bagel Bites Café for lunch around one o'clock?"

That gave her three hours. Which should be enough. "Sure."

Holly galloped down the stairs. There were fresh muffins on the table, which made her suspect that Jake had already been over this morning, plus a glass of juice that was probably meant for her. While she ate, she checked back in her notes. She'd heard parts of her mother and Jake's conversation during the drive home yesterday, and she agreed with them. Rose couldn't have shot that gun. It didn't make sense.

So who had Conrad Beckett seen at the window?

Holly found the background notes she'd been thinking of and underlined the relevant portion, pressing down hard on her pen in her excitement. *This* made so much more sense. Everyone would be so impressed when she told them. She'd cracked this case, and she'd done it almost all on her own.

Only one thing bothered her. Her solution was logical and it fit all the facts. But was there enough evidence for a conviction? She'd learned from Kelly that it wasn't enough to *know* someone had committed a crime. You had to be able to *prove* it in court.

The letter from Conrad Beckett wouldn't be sufficient—especially since one of his conclusions was wrong. The notes she'd just read from the newspaper article probably wouldn't do it, either.

Which meant she had to find something else. She already had an idea where to start looking. Thinking ahead, she planned what she might need. A plastic bag, so she could protect anything she found from her fingerprints, a camera…maybe that tiny tape recorder of hers, too.

Holly went back upstairs to organize everything into her backpack. She made sure the batteries in the camera and the recorder were both working. Then she called goodbye to her mother and slipped out the front door. She was already on her scooter when she remembered she'd left her notebook on the kitchen table. That was okay. She wouldn't need it.

MAUREEN FINISHED A PHONE call at twelve-forty-five and decided against making another. She didn't want to be late for her lunch with Holly. After stopping at the bathroom mirror to brush her hair and put on her foundation and lipstick, she ran down the stairs and grabbed her purse out of the closet.

The gleaming silver of her new scooter caught her eye.

Should she?

It was a lovely day and Holly would get a kick

out of seeing her mother scoot up to the restaurant in this. But Maureen wasn't in the right frame of mind. She couldn't get over her conversation with Holly yesterday.

She'd thought about it all last night, and intermittently this morning. What it boiled down to was that she hadn't been there for her daughter during the darkest moment of her life. She'd hung back, emotionally, so afraid of rejection she hadn't realized what her daughter needed most.

She was ashamed of herself and terribly afraid that a turnaround now was going to be too little, too late.

Still, Holly had agreed to this lunch, so that was a good sign.

Take the scooter, Maureen. Make an effort.

With a sigh, she hauled it out of the closet, through the front door, down the small landing. As she zipped along the curve of the cul de sac, she felt a small tug of physical joy. This *was* fun. Maybe she and Holly could have a little race after their lunch.

WHEN HOLLY WASN'T AT the Bagel Bites Café by ten after one, Maureen was annoyed. By twenty after, she was worried. She scootered back to the town house and tried calling her sisters. Neither of them had heard from Holly.

Maureen tapped her index finger on the glass tabletop. If the half-eaten muffin next to the drained glass of juice was the sum total of Holly's breakfast, she had to be starving by now. So why hadn't she shown up for lunch? Next to the muffin was a notebook of Holly's. Desperate, Maureen glanced at it.

It was a casebook, she realized after a few moments, with entries carefully dated and sources noted. Her gaze caught by some black underscoring, Maureen read a passage that had been copied from the *Canmore Leader* in October 1999. At first the single sentence appeared innocuous. Then Linda Beckett's disclosures of the previous day came back to her and she gasped.

Oh, my God. Was Holly following up on this on her own?

Maureen grabbed her cell phone out of her purse, even as she rushed to her car. Damn it, Jake wasn't home. She'd have to leave a message.

"Jake, it's Maureen. Holly's missing—I think she's playing private detective again, only I'm worried she might actually be on to something. In her notebook I found some notes from the *Leader* about the night Jilly was murdered. Do you remember who was in the kitchen, helping Rose that night?"

Maureen paused, thinking of the implications, and wondering just how daring Holly would be in verifying this information. If only she'd come to *her* with this. Or the police.

Before hanging up, she added, "I'm going to try to find her. I'll call again when I know more."

CHAPTER SIXTEEN

HOLLY COULDN'T BELIEVE her luck when she found the door to Beth Gibson's real estate firm unlocked. The man who shared the business with Beth was in his office, on the phone. He didn't see her come in, or notice her creep down to the second door, which also turned out to be unlocked.

Safely inside, Holly was surprised to see almost a dozen cardboard boxes stacked against the wall. Closed with packing tape, they were labeled to be delivered to the Thunder Bar M ranch. That was Dylan's ranch—or it had been before his mother married Max Strongman.

Thoroughly puzzled, Holly scanned the rest of the room. Beth's desk was clear—only a phone sat on the polished surface. The drawers of an adjacent cabinet were all ajar. Holly checked—sure enough they were all empty.

So Beth was clearing out of her office. Why? The reason was probably important, but Holly didn't have time to work it out. She had to be really fast.

Examining the boxes closer, she was relieved to see that the contents were labeled. Many of them contained office supplies, old real estate files, useless stuff.

Holly knew businesses had to keep their receipts and stuff for several years for income tax reasons. Was it too much to hope that Beth's papers from her old catering business might be here, too?

If she could just find the invoice for that night at the Strongmans', then she could prove Beth had been in the kitchen with Rose Strongman that night. And who knows, she might find something else, too.

Cautiously, Holly shifted the top boxes to the floor. More real estate files…darn. Then, finally, at almost the last box she saw the label she'd been praying for. Gourmet Grub, Catering Co. Holly used the point of a pen to tear away the packing tape. Inside were invoices and expense receipts organized by date and by function. Johnston's Fortieth Birthday Party, March 13, 1999. She was at the right year, at least.

She flipped forward, past the spring and summer months to the fall. Finally, she was at the very last packet in the box. Hoping desperately, she peeked at the label. Thunder Bar M Barbecue, October 8, 1999.

This was it! Beth Gibson *had* been the caterer. Holly scanned the itemized invoice, noting that the Strongmans had been billed for four hours of on-site preparation at fifteen dollars an hour. She took a few photographs, then stuck the papers back into the box, closed the lid...

And tried the very last box. Here were bank statements. Holly knew how these worked. Her mother had set her up with checking and savings accounts when she turned ten. She decided to trace the receipt of that last invoice. Sure enough, the exact amount had been deposited in October. Something else was interesting, too. A very large check written that same month.

Holly went through the stacks of canceled checks. And there it was. Made out to James Strongman.

This had to be important. She snapped another picture and had just put her camera back into her pack, when the door to the office closed.

Holly jumped, then slammed the cardboard lid down on the box. Beth Gibson glared at her.

"Holly?"

"I—I'm sorry, Mrs. Gibson. I know I shouldn't be here...." She scrambled to her feet and edged for the door.

Beth intercepted her, grabbing her arm.

"I have to go! I'm supposed to meet my mom...."

"I don't think so." Beth took something out of her purse. Holly gasped when she saw the gun.

"I'm sorry. I didn't find anything. Honest, I didn't!" The expression on Beth's face scared her almost more than the gun. No question now that this woman was the one. What had seemed like a game, an interesting challenge, was suddenly, paralyzingly, real. Jeez, why hadn't she been more careful?

She shot a glance past the open door to the hallway. If she screamed for help...

"We're alone now, Holly. Philip has gone for lunch. So it won't do any good to cry out. Because I guarantee no one will hear a damn thing."

Beth shoved the end of the gun right against Holly's ribs. It hurt.

Mom! Aunt Kelly! Oh, how was anyone going to help her when no one knew where she was? That she could die here, right now, made her feel as if her body had frozen from the inside out.

What was Beth planning to do? Holly could tell the older woman was running through her options. She was frowning, eyes narrowed, toe tapping against the low pile carpet.

"I guess I'll have to take you out to the ranch," she said finally. "This time let's see if Max has any brilliant ideas."

IT TOOK MAUREEN LESS THAN a minute to drive back downtown. In that time she managed to get hold of Kelly, who'd gone into Calgary to shop for Billy's upcoming birthday. She was on her way back now, having aborted those plans out of concern for her niece.

"Have you found Holly yet?" she asked.

"No, but I have a good idea where to look."
Maureen told her about the quote from the newspaper.

"Yes, Beth *was* the caterer," Kelly confirmed. "I
think it was the last job she ever took on. Her van
was parked round the side of the house, by the door
that leads to the kitchen, when we arrived that night.
Poor Rose practically had a breakdown and Beth
was trying to calm her when we went in to get their
statements."

"Can you remember what each woman said?"

"Not word for word, but the gist. According to
Rose, she was in the washroom when the firecracker
went off. When she came out, Beth told her that
someone had been shot and they'd better call the
ambulance."

"Could Beth have been the one?" Maureen
asked.

"It's certainly possible. She said she was in the
kitchen at the time, tossing salads. But with Rose in
the washroom, she could've easily snuck into the
dining room for a few minutes."

"That's what I thought. And I think Holly's on
the same track. Hopefully she isn't foolish enough
to confront Beth...." Maureen tightened her fingers
on the steering wheel.

"She's probably out with her friends, having so
much fun she forgot about her plans to meet you for
lunch."

"Oh, I hope so!" Maureen braked in front of the Gibsons' rustic-looking A-frame. "I have to go now, Kel. I'm at Beth's."

"Okay. I should be there in about half an hour."

Thank God for cell phones! Maureen tucked hers back in her purse and dashed out of the car. She'd half expected to see Holly's scooter on the Gibsons' landing and was disappointed when she didn't.

Alan Gibson opened the door after her fourth knock. He appeared absolutely bagged: unshaven, unshowered, exhausted.

"Do I know you?" he asked, rubbing his eyes.

"I'm sorry to interrupt. I'm Maureen Shannon and I'm looking for my daughter, Holly. I thought she might have dropped in to talk to your wife."

"Beth?" Alan put a hand out to the door frame to steady himself. "Well, she wouldn't find her here. My wife left me last night. Just out of the blue. Told me she wanted a divorce. Later this afternoon a moving truck is coming...God!" He covered his face with his free hand and his shoulders shook.

"Sorry," he murmured. "Must still be in shock."

And maybe a little drunk, too. Maureen could smell stale alcohol as she followed the man by the arm and led him inside. The family room was tidy, freshly vacuumed and dusted. The only sign of disarray were two empty six-packs of beer next to the reclining chair. If Alan had spent the past twelve hours falling apart—and he probably had—he'd managed to do it very neatly.

"Alan, let me call someone for you. One of your sons, maybe? Or a friend?"

"Not yet," he pleaded. "I can't face anyone until I pull myself together. It still hasn't sunk in. Beth worked crazy hours, what with being an alderwoman and having a real estate business. I never guessed she was having an affair, too."

So he knew that much of the truth, at least. Maureen was afraid that other shocks lay in store. But right now, her main concern was Holly. "Did Beth tell you where she was going?"

Bitterness turned down the corners of his mouth. "Moving into the house on the Thunder Bar M with Max Strongman. She's quitting her job—I guess with Strongman's money she won't need to work." His face wrinkled in disgust. "The dirty bastard...when I get my hands on him..."

Maureen didn't believe Alan's threats were serious. Still, she cautioned him not to overreact. "Beth's the loser in this scenario, not you. In a day or so you'll see what I mean."

ON HER WAY TO THE THUNDER Bar M, Maureen phoned Kelly, letting her know the change in plans, then Jake. He was back from running some banking errands and had just listened to her first message.

"Would Holly really follow up a hunch like this on her own?" he asked.

Maureen didn't bother to answer. She *knew* Holly would do exactly that. "I'm on my way to the Thunder Bar M. Beth left her husband last night. If she has Holly, that's probably where she'll take her."

Because of the isolation. God, it was a scary, scary thought. Surely Beth wouldn't harm a young girl like Holly. *But if she'd killed Jilly Beckett...*

Maureen pressed on the accelerator to avoid a red light. Hitting the highway was a relief, because she could go as fast as she dared here. A hundred and thirty, a hundred and forty kilometers an hour, was way over the speed limit, but when every minute might be the minute she was too late by, it still wasn't enough.

The steering wheel jerked in Maureen's hand when she took the corner to the graveled access road. Bypassing the turnoff to the B and B, she drove on to the wrought-iron gates of the Thunder Bar M. Atypically, the entranceway was barred. She jumped out of the BMW to check if the gates were locked. Sure enough, a shiny new padlock was securely fastened.

So she'd have to go on foot. Taking only her cell phone with her, Maureen left her car unlocked and began to run along the packed dirt road. She had about a quarter of a mile to plan what she was going to do when she got to the ranch house. The only element she had going for her at this point was surprise. Thank heavens Max didn't own a dog.

"WHAT DO YOU MEAN, *this is our problem now?*" Max Strongman was pacing the living room in the old ranch house.

Holly shivered on the sofa where Beth had told her to sit. Although it was sunny and warm outside, the shade of a nearby grove of aspen kept the interior of the log house cool. And she was dressed in only a pair of shorts and a T-shirt. So far no one had tied her up, or hit her, or done anything really freaky like that. But Beth still had that gun in her hands. Which was terrifying enough.

"I've taken care of all the sticky problems up till now. Frankly, I'm sick of it. This one you can handle."

"Beth, have you gone crazy? Why is this girl a problem to us?"

The real estate agent—*Max's lover*—was getting more and more frazzled by the minute. Her hair, which was usually sprayed perfectly into place, looked windblown. Her face had gone pale, with just two red dots of color on her cheeks.

"I told you, she found my catering receipt for that night!"

"So what? The police already know that you were there. They took your statement, along with the rest of us."

"Yes. But the police don't know about the payment I made to James. *She* found the canceled check."

Max stopped pacing. The buckle on his belt caught a ray of light from the window and reflected right back into Holly's eyes. "What the hell are you talking about?"

"I paid James to set off that firecracker. I told him to consider it an advance, that when the oil deal went through there'd be plenty more where that came from. He was only too pleased to help his daddy get what you both wanted."

"You put him up to that scheme? Did you get him the gun, too?"

Beth made an impatient sound. "James didn't *shoot* anyone. It was me, Max. God, I thought you *knew*. I did it for you, Max, and for us and our boys...."

"But *why?*"

"Don't you remember talking to James and me before the barbecue? You told us you were afraid Dylan might organize a protest and rally public opinion to his side of the issue. Also, you were afraid Beckett was getting cold feet about the deal. We solved both those problems for you that night. For a while everyone blamed Dylan and all the heat was off your deal. Beckett was so broken up about his kid that he stepped right out of the business, and the remaining directors were only too pleased to sign off on your contract.''

''It really *was* you.'' Strongman stared at her, amazed.

Beth looked sickeningly pleased with herself. ''Everything would've been perfect if I'd been able to complete my plan and hide the gun in Dylan's truck. But I made the mistake of entrusting that detail to your son.''

Max backed up a step. ''What did you ask James to do?''

''I gave him the gun and told him to put it in a safe place, where the police wouldn't find it. He threw it in the damned river, where *nobody* could ever find it! If he hadn't done that, my plan would've been perfect. Your stepson would be in jail right now, and I might not have had to kill Rose.''

''You killed my wife, too?'' Max took another step backward. From his expression, he was just as shocked as Holly felt.

''Did I have a choice? You knew she was going to change her will. Didn't you overhear her talking to that accountant?''

''Yes, but I— Oh, God, Beth. I just can't believe this. No wonder you were so quick to offer me that alibi. You were really just protecting yourself.''

Holly wrapped her arms around her chest and tried to will her body to stop shaking. Beth was a freaking monster. How was she ever going to escape? No way could she dash for the door. Beth would shoot her without even caring.

And then her mom would be all alone, just like Linda Beckett was. Holly felt a tear drip onto her arm, but didn't look or try to wipe her eyes. As much as possible, she had to blend into the background. Maybe they'd get so worked up between the two of them that they'd forget she was here....

"But what about James?" Max had his voice back under control now. "Don't tell me he planted that gun under Dylan's mattress to cover up *your* crime?"

"I may have done the actual shooting, but James and I were in this together. Don't forget, your son was counting on a big inheritance. He didn't want that will changed any more than I did."

"But if he didn't kill anyone, why did he ask for me to help him leave the country?"

"Come on, Max. James didn't pull any triggers, but he couldn't prove that, could he? I helped him see that avoiding the police was his only option. Frankly, Max, I couldn't count on your son not to give me away. He's not too bright, I'm afraid."

"No, he isn't," Max said. "And you took full advantage of that fact, didn't you."

"Don't blame me because James gave himself away. I had everything set up perfectly to frame Dylan. Even had it arranged so that he was seen leaving his mother's house at just the right time. But again, James messed up on a simple matter like planting the murder weapon."

Max had backed himself against the wall now. There was no place else for him to go as Beth kept moving toward him.

"So what do you want me to do?" he said finally, his eyes on the gun in her hand.

"You take care of this kid, then we're home free. We'll get married like you wanted us to, and go ahead with our development plans. We'll turn this tired ranch into a deluxe vacation resort, just like you always dreamed."

"But what about my son? All this was supposed to be for James, for his children. I wanted to build something real, something that would last. But James has no future now."

"Don't forget about my sons, Max," Beth said, her voice as smooth as the leather on the couch Holly was sitting on. "We can leave the money and the land to them."

AT THE OPEN WINDOW MAUREEN could hear everything. Sneaking a glance, she spied Beth with a gun. Max cowered near a wall. Where was Holly? Maybe she wasn't there... But wait. Maureen spotted her daughter's scooter on the floor. Then heard a muffled sob from inside the room. *Oh, Holly...*

Maureen ducked her head as she tried to decide what to do.

"You'll have to take care of the girl," she heard Beth say.

Maureen's throat closed over a lump of pure, unadulterated hate. If she had a gun in her hand she would shoot the woman in a heartbeat. But she was pathetically ill-equipped to protect her daughter. All she could do was stall them and hope Kelly arrived in time.

She went round to the front door and tested the handle. Unlocked. One turn of the knob, a gentle push, and she was in. To her left was the door to the dining room, as Jake had described it. To the right, the large living room, where Beth had her little girl.

Maureen considered her options, and realized she had none. Hoping not to startle anyone into overreacting, she spoke quietly.

"There you are, Holly. I've been searching everywhere for you."

Beth swiveled, then swore. Max stepped away from the wall, brushing his hands over the sides of his trousers. The smile of relief on Holly's face was so full of trust and faith Maureen felt like crying. Too bad she was about to let her daughter down even worse than she had in the past. It was terrible seeing the hope in her daughter's face die as she realized her mother was unarmed and unaccompanied.

Beth raised her gun as she comprehended the same facts. "Maureen, I'm sure your mother raised you to phone before you dropped in for a visit."

"Beth, put that gun away. Don't be a fool." Feeling fearless—because if Holly was hurt, what else could ever matter—Maureen went straight to her daughter. Holly's arms around her neck were the only reality worth knowing in this godforsaken room.

"You're the fool, Maureen. You know we can't let you leave—neither of you." Beth moved quickly, blocking the doorway.

"Max, don't let her make you a part of this," Maureen begged. "Believe me, the RCMP are on their way. If you hurt Holly or me, you won't get away with it." She pushed her daughter behind her, shielding her body.

Holly was leaning against her and trembling. Poor baby was scared to death. Maureen reached back to stroke her cold, fragile arm, and tried to calculate how long it would take Kelly to get here. Five more minutes? Ten?

"She's right, Beth." Max's voice was as gravelly as the road Maureen had raced along to get here. "You shoot these people and it's all over."

Beth swung the gun from Maureen to her lover. "I'm not shooting anyone. I told you, this time it's your turn. And we don't need to use the gun. I figure an accident on the river would be the best. Hurry!'' She jostled the gun in Maureen's direction again. ''Outside. You have a canoe, Max. That ought to work.''

As they were being ushered out of the house, Maureen's cell phone began to ring. Beth glowered at her, then held out her hand. Maureen pulled the slim model out of the pocket of her shirt, making sure to hit the Talk button.

''That gun makes you pretty brave, doesn't it, Beth?'' she yelled, hoping whoever was calling would hear.

''Bloody contraptions!'' Beth tossed the plastic case into the middle of the aspens.

''That was probably my sister, telling me she's almost here,'' Maureen improvised.

God, please let it be true! How had Holly ended up in this situation? Maureen prayed she'd have the opportunity to hear the whole story.

They were out on the porch now. At one time the cedar structure must have been impressive, but neglect and time had resulted in several rotted spots. Maureen was careful where she stepped as she emerged from the door.

''Hurry up,'' Beth urged.

Maureen found she just couldn't. ''Go to hell, Beth. My daughter and I aren't going along with any plan of yours.''

Unexpectedly, Beth raised a foot and kicked her. Maureen stumbled and almost fell.

"Don't underestimate me, Maureen. That would be a big mistake."

Fear mixed with disbelief. Part of her just couldn't accept that this woman was for real. But the gun was genuine. The two murders had been real. With Holly here, she couldn't afford to take any chances.

"Let my daughter go, at least. She's just a kid."

"Yeah. Some kid. Following me around like a regular private detective." She focused on Holly. "Snooping on me and Max, too."

"S-sorry," Holly whispered.

"What the hell am I going to do with the two of you?" Beth shifted the position of the gun in her hand.

It was heavy, Maureen realized. *Her arm was getting tired.*

"Maybe I should just shoot you both now, and be done with it," Beth said suddenly. "Max can get rid of your bodies later."

She raised her gun again. God, she was really going to do it! Maureen threw herself in front of Holly. In the same instant she heard her sister's cry.

"Drop your gun, Beth!"

Kelly emerged from the brush along the side of the road, her own Smith & Wesson out in front of her.

Max swore. "You idiot," he said to Beth. "Now what're you going to do? Shoot the cop, too?"

"Shut up!" Beth shrieked. She tried to grab Holly's arm, but Maureen wasn't budging. Finally Beth gave up and clenched Maureen's wrist, pressing the gun to her ribs.

Kelly stopped advancing. Maureen could almost see the sweat break out over her skin. Her sister was in the same situation she'd faced with Cathleen and Danny Mizzoni, less than a year ago. A situation that had taken her to the brink of hell and beyond.

Despite the danger to herself, and her worry about Holly, Maureen felt desperately for her sister. *God, don't make her choose again. This is too much to ask of one human being.*

And then something—no, *someone*—was flying out the front door behind them.

"Jake!"

He tackled Beth; her gun fell to the rotting porch. Kelly moved quickly to cover Max, while Maureen scurried to capture the weapon. Meanwhile, Jake continued to pin Beth down.

"Check her for other weapons, Jake. You." Kelly gestured at Max. "Get down on the porch floor. Now!"

Maureen passed Beth's gun to her sister. "You all right?"

Kelly nodded. "Look after Holly. Jake and I have this under control."

Holly. She was standing where Maureen had left her, still trembling, pale, eyes unfocused. Maureen gathered her into her arms and stroked her silky hair.

"Are you okay, Holly? Oh, my God, if that woman hurt you…" She pressed Holly's hands with her own, as she visually inspected her daughter's face. She ran her hands up her arms and around to her back.

"M-Mom…" Holly was trembling so hard Maureen decided to carry her. It wasn't easy, but she needed to get her child out of there.

Max and Beth were on the floor of the porch now. Kelly held both guns, while Jake ran into the house to see if he could find some rope.

Maureen set Holly down on a patch of grass some distance from the house and collapsed beside her. "It's okay, baby. You're going to be okay." At some point, she must have started crying, because her tears were dripping off her face, falling on her daughter's white T-shirt, making blotchy gray stains.

"You co-could've died, Mom. I'm so-sorry."

"Oh, Holly." Maureen wrapped her in a hug. "I'm just so thankful that your aunt arrived in time."

If she hadn't… This situation—it was all her fault. She should have put a stop to Holly's amateur sleuthing weeks ago…when she'd found out that Holly had taken snapshots of Beth and Max. That would have been the perfect time to confiscate her detecting kit and forbid her to go anywhere near Beth or Max.

That was what she *should* have done. And what *had* she done? She'd taken her daughter along to Linda Beckett's house yesterday, *fostering* her interest in the case.

And hand-delivering the final piece of the puzzle that had led Holly to Beth.

Even this morning, when Holly had said she was going downtown, Maureen had just blithely given her permission, when she should have known her daughter well enough to sense something was up.

It was negligence, pure and simple, Maureen realized.

"Did you call for backup?" Jake asked Kelly as he helped bind Beth's arms behind her back.

"I did," Kelly confirmed. "Springer should be here shortly. He was a bit shocked to hear Beth was behind everything, let me tell you."

It was Max's turn to be tied. Jake was none too gentle in securing the knots. Maureen saw the older man grimace, but he didn't complain.

"How did you get inside the house?" Kelly asked Jake.

"I arrived just a minute after you. I saw you running up the lane ahead of me and decided to make a wide loop and come through the rear of the house. The kitchen door was unlocked, and I heard voices out on the porch."

Jake backed away from the trussed-up couple on the floor and started toward the grassy patch where Maureen still held her daughter. His expression as he crouched beside them was pure tenderness. He put a hand on each of their shoulders.

"You okay, kid?"

Holly sniffled and nodded.

"And you, Maureen?"

She couldn't answer, couldn't meet his gaze. She'd stopped crying, but now her body was shaking, worse than Holly's.

The high-pitched wail of sirens became audible and Jake sighed with relief. "It's going to be so good to see those two cuffed in the back of a squad car."

"I-is Kelly okay?" Maureen stammered over the question. She could see that her baby sister was still up by the house, her gun trained on the two suspects.

"Maureen, your sister is just fine. She handled the entire situation like a pro."

Holly wormed out of her mother's arms. She'd been recovering steadily since Beth and Max were immobilized. She'd stopped trembling and her skin had warmed quickly out in the sun.

"Did you hear any of the things Beth said, Jake?" she asked.

He shook his head.

"She confessed to almost everything. She shot

Jilly Beckett and Rose Strongman with James's help. And guess what?'' She nudged the pack that still hung off her fragile shoulders. ''I have every word she said on tape.''

CHAPTER SEVENTEEN

WITH MAX AND BETH CUFFED and on their way to the RCMP detachment, Jake had hoped the trouble was over. But on the ride home, with Maureen in the front beside him and Holly in the back seat of his truck, he knew that it had just started.

Maureen was in shock. Definitely, she was in no condition to drive. They'd left her BMW parked in front of the Thunder Bar M gates, the keys in the ignition. Cathleen and Dylan were going to drive it into Canmore later that evening.

Still pale and shaky, Maureen spoke only once for the duration of the trip, to ask a question. "Where's Kelly?"

Jake met the reflection of Holly's eyes in the rear view mirror. "She's gone to the detachment to help deal with Max and Beth."

Kelly had taken Holly's camera and tape recording of Beth's conversation with Max. Jake could tell that Holly felt pretty good about her contribution to the arrest. She'd recovered from her big scare quickly. But now, as she nibbled the corner of her lower lip and shot worried glances at her mom, he figured she was calculating the price of her adventure.

At the town house, Jake encouraged Maureen to sit on the back deck in the sun. When she still couldn't seem to stop trembling, he brought out a blanket and a glass of her brandy.

"Try this." He handed her the snifter, then crouched beside her. "Pretty scary, huh?"

She didn't say anything, just kept staring off into the distance. Not at the view, not at anything.

"Where's Holly?" she finally asked.

"She said she was hungry. I think she's warming up some soup. Do you want anything?"

Maureen shook her head.

Sandwiching one of her hands, he rubbed at her skin as if she had frostbite. But he knew the chill came from inside her, from a different kind of coldness.

She didn't respond to his touch, didn't even look at him.

"I almost lost you today." Saying the words brought home the truth of it. In a rush, he felt all that she'd come to mean to him. Her ability to bring him to his knees with one insightful comment, one stroke of her tennis racket, one lingering kiss...

He pressed his lips to the hand he'd been stroking, then brushed the back of his fingers down the side of her face. Her only reaction was a blink.

"Oh, Maureen." Had she heard a word he'd said?

Did she have any idea what he'd gone through today? "You know, I was a perfectly happy bachelor until you came along. Now the very idea of being without you scares me more than my own death ever could."

He felt the pressure of her fingers squeezing his. Tears pooled in her eyes but didn't fall.

She *was* listening, at least.

"I know this timing is terrible, but since I'm down on my knees, anyway…" He paused, hoping she would smile, even though the joke was lame. When she didn't, he took a deep breath and carried on.

"Would you do me the honor of marrying me, Maureen? I promise you my love and my faithfulness. I'll cherish and protect you and Holly as long as I live."

What else could he offer? He wanted to give her everything. All that had been missing in her marriage to Rod. All that she could possibly dream of for her future.

"We could have another child, if you'd like," he said tentatively. "Maybe two…"

A sob escaped from her lips. She covered her mouth and closed her eyes as a little breeze kicked up the strands of her hair and sent some dried leaves on the deck tumbling into the corner by the wall. He felt her shiver, and he pulled the blanket higher around her shoulders.

The sun had settled into the lower quadrant of the sky now, and the birds were becoming a little more active. A curious whiskey jack landed on the wooden railing, tilted his head at them, then flew off.

"What an idiot I am," Jake said, slowly rising to a standing position, unable to bear the aching in his knee joints any longer. "Proposing to you an hour after you've faced down an armed madwoman." He went to the railing, planted his hands on the solid wood and pretended he was admiring the view. In truth, he saw little other than his own insensitivity.

Had he thought his proposal, like the prince's magical kiss, could wake the sleeping princess?

"Jake, that was the sweetest proposal I could imagine."

He turned slowly and found her round eyes in focus now, honing in on him. His heart came back to life, thumping in his chest like a beaver's tail on water.

"Will you, Maureen? Marry me?"

IN A FEW YEARS she would look back on this day and consider it the craziest of her life. Maureen shifted her gaze past Jake to the mountains and did her best to dissemble. If she'd processed everything he'd said correctly, Jake had just asked her to marry him.

He couldn't mean it, of course. He was just being

kind. The way he'd been the last time she broke down in front of him.

Some men were like that—they turned to mush when they saw a woman cry. And maybe right now Jake really did believe he loved her and wanted to marry her. But once life returned to normal around here—assuming it ever could—he'd regret the offer he'd just made.

"Jake, this isn't the time…"

"Maybe not. But now that I've asked, you're not going to leave me dangling. If you don't love me, then say so. I'll appreciate the honesty."

If you don't love me. But she did, Maureen realized. She *did* love him. God help her, she was *crazy* about this man. He was great with Holly, and even more important, he was great with *her.*

"Please, Maureen…"

She couldn't look at him. Why was he pressing her like this? To just give in and say yes was so tempting. But being weak wasn't the answer. "Thanks for asking, Jake. But we both know marriage isn't what either of us wants."

"It isn't?"

She shook her head and, avoiding his outstretched hand, escaped down the steps from the deck to the path that led to the creek.

Past the small lawn, the landscape was wild. She picked her way through the tangles of wild grasses and weeds until she came to the rocky border of the creek. Through the thin soles of her shoes, she could feel the hard shapes of the stones. She walked until water was lapping over her toes, then stopped.

Jake followed behind her. She could hear the swish of his feet in the grass and the crunching sound as he crossed over the rocks.

Finally, he caught up to her.

"Is it the idea of marriage you're opposed to? Or just marriage to me?"

"You don't know what you risk getting into. I was as bad at being a wife as I am at being a mother. The problems between me and Rod weren't all his fault."

This was hard to admit. For years she'd trained herself to see only Rod's bad points, never the positive attributes that had drawn her to him in the first place.

"I told myself it was because of Rod and his expensive tastes that I had to put so many hours into my career, but the truth is that I enjoyed my work and took satisfaction from it. It was me, not Rod, who was responsible for allowing my relationship with Holly to deteriorate. Oh, I always justified my absences by telling myself that Holly really preferred her father, anyway."

"Maureen—"

"What Rod said to me that night before he left for South America was true, too. I *was* a shrew to him. I always nagged, always found fault. I blamed him for making me behave that way, but I had a choice, Jake. I contributed to the failure of our marriage just as much as he did.''

''Okay, you made mistakes. Now you can learn from them and go on....''

Oh, he made it sound so simple! ''Jake, I can't argue with you about this anymore. I've told you my decision. That's the way it has to be.'' As long as she wasn't looking at him, it was possible for her to say the necessary words. Resolutely, she kept staring out over the creek at the mountains, until she finally sensed him moving away from her.

She listened to his footsteps as he stepped over the stones, and then through the grass. Heard him ascend the wooden stairs, step by step. When she was certain he was gone, she buried her face in her hands and wept.

''MOM? ARE YOU OUT THERE?''

It was fifteen minutes later, maybe twenty. Maureen was sitting unceremoniously at the water's edge, tossing pebbles into the water, then watching them sink.

''Down here, Holly. By the creek.''

''What're you doing? You'll get all wet....''

Maureen's lips were so dry it hurt to smile. If Holly had any idea who she sounded like, she'd be mortified. ''I'm all right.'' She stood, then brushed rock dust from her clothes.

"Aunt Cathleen just called. She and Dylan will be bringing back our car in about an hour. Poppy's coming with them and she's cooking us dinner. Cathleen wondered if we should invite Kelly and her family, too, because Kelly will probably be too exhausted to cook and Mick had the kids at the office…"

The whole gang at her house for dinner? Maureen shrugged. Maybe the commotion would stop her from stewing about the big mess she'd made of her life.

"Is—is Jake still around?"

"No. He's gone home. Said we should call him if we need him. Do you want me to invite him to dinner, too?"

In normal circumstances, she would. She had much to thank him for. Saving her daughter. Saving her. But given their last conversation, a dinner invitation would definitely not be appropriate. "I don't think so."

Holly paused a long moment, then nodded. "I'll just call Mick, then."

Two hours later, the entire Shannon clan had assembled in the small town house. Poppy rustled up pasta and salad in the kitchen—Holly's favorite meal. Dylan busied himself by doing mundane jobs like adding salt to the water softener and checking to make sure the new dryer was venting properly.

In the living room, Amanda, pretending to be a

hairdresser, stuck numerous barrettes and ribbons into Mick's hair, while Holly, Kelly, Cathleen and Billy played a round of Yahtzee.

Maureen watched Holly roll the dice...

"Two more sixes. Great! I'll use it for my four of a kind."

...then wandered back to the kitchen. She couldn't stand still, and she couldn't focus on any one job for more than a few minutes at a time.

Coming back to her original task, which was to set the larger table in the dining room, she counted out napkins and forks. "Let's see, Holly and me, that's two. Add Kelly's family, makes six, then Dylan, Cathleen and you, Poppy, and we're at nine."

From her position at the stove, stirring the tomato sauce, Poppy asked, "Jake isn't joining us?"

Maureen stared down at the neat pile of linen napkins and gleaming stainless steel. "No. He isn't."

"I hear he saved your life. Yours and Holly's."

"Yes, he was wonderful," Maureen said quickly. She met her grandmother's eyes. "He asked me to marry him this afternoon. And I said no."

For a long moment, the older woman regarded her. Then finally she sighed sadly. "I see. I'm very sorry to hear that."

Maureen didn't ask what she was sorry about. The topic wasn't open for discussion. Not even with Poppy, this time.

"The sauce is ready, Maureen. Will you call everyone to dinner?"

Poppy's meal was simple but as delicious as everything she made. After, they all crowded into the living room to watch a cartoon video. *The Adventurers Down Under* had Billy and Amanda laughing so hard they were much more entertaining than the movie.

When it was over, at nine o'clock, Kelly insisted they had to go.

"Look at poor Amanda. She can hardly stand on her two feet."

Mick whisked the little girl up on his shoulders and Kelly took Billy's hand. Once they'd left, Cathleen, Dylan and Poppy followed. All too soon, only Holly and Maureen remained.

"It's so quiet," Holly said, toeing the edge of the rug in the hallway.

"Time to go to bed, Holly."

"Aw, Mom, it's only *nine!*"

"Please don't argue. Not after the day we just went through." Maureen ran both of her hands through her hair and wondered if there was a muscle in her body that wasn't aching.

"Okay." Reluctantly, Holly headed for the stairs.

"I'll come and check on you in ten minutes."

"I'm not a—" Abruptly she cut off her own sentence. She paused a moment, then said quietly, "Thanks."

Cathleen and Kelly had left her kitchen so clean Maureen couldn't find even one small job to occupy herself as she waited to say good-night to Holly. She wondered what impulse had prompted her daughter to choke back that reminder that she wasn't a baby. Whatever the reason, she was thankful for it.

The living room was just as tidy as the kitchen. The Yahtzee game had been put away in the drawer of the entertainment unit; the video had been returned to its case and filed alphabetically with the others in their small movie collection.

Maureen went to close the blinds and paused as her gaze fell on the river. What was Jake doing right now?

She couldn't stand to think about it. Instead, she counted off the remaining two minutes on her watch and then climbed the stairs.

Holly was already under her covers, with the bear Cathleen had said she could keep from the B and B tucked in beside her. After smoothing out a corner of the duvet, Maureen sat.

"That was a scary experience you went through today, Holly. I hope you don't have nightmares, but if you do I want you to wake me, okay?"

Holly nodded. After a few moments of silence, she asked hesitantly, "Are you mad?"

"No. Not at you." Maureen brushed the hair back from Holly's forehead. "At myself. I shouldn't have let your investigation go so far. I don't think I quite realized how serious you were.''

"I want to be a detective when I grow up."

She sounded so defiant. Maureen sighed. "It can be a dangerous job."

"I'll be smarter next time."

"Next time better be after you've finished the RCMP training program in Regina," Maureen cautioned her.

Holly had the sense to look abashed. "Yeah. Aunt Kelly already talked to me. She said I was clever to realize the murderer was Beth, but that I should've taken my ideas to her. The police could've found the same evidence I did, without putting anyone's life in danger."

Maureen smiled. "You *were* clever." She bent to kiss her daughter on the cheek and was gratified when Holly gave her a big hug in return.

AFTER HER MOTHER LEFT her room, Holly could hear her wandering around the house. The sounds were vaguely comforting as she drifted off to sleep. A few hours later, she woke up suddenly. The clock read one in the morning.

She hadn't had a nightmare. What had disturbed her? Then she heard it again, muffled crying.

Oh, no. Her mother. The guilt she'd been feeling earlier came back and landed like one big heap of dough at the bottom of her stomach.

Holly crept out of bed and into slippers and a robe. At the door she paused. All the lights were out, except for the faint, golden glow from her mother's bedroom. She crept along the hallway, careful not to make a sound. At the closed door, she decided not to knock but instead slipped quietly into the room.

Her mom was on the chaise longue in the corner. She had a book facedown in her lap and a box of tissues by her side. Judging from her face, she'd been sobbing for a while.

"Holly." Her mom straightened her back and wiped the most recent tears from her face. "Did you have a bad dream?"

"No." She perched on the edge of the chair and reached out for the hem of her mother's flannel housecoat. The old fabric was so soft and thin. "You're crying," she said, knowing it was a stupid thing to say.

Her mother smiled and nodded. "It's been one of those days."

"I'm really sorry, Mom." And she was. Her mother had stepped in front of Beth's gun just to protect her. If Beth had pulled the trigger, her mom could've *died*.

"I know, sweetie."

"I'm sorry about more than just today." It was hard to say what was on her mind without being disloyal to her dad. She'd loved him so much. But he hadn't been fair to her mother. And neither had she.

"What are you sorry about?"

"Dad and I were always leaving you out of things. I felt so special that Dad wanted to be with me, but I never thought how you must've felt." Her dad had made it into a game. *Don't tell Mom. She'd never let us do it. This is just between you and me, angel.*

"We were mean, Mom. And I'm sorry." Now she was crying, too. Her mother pulled her close and stroked her head. Holly found herself remembering the scent of her perfume from long ago, back when her mother had tucked her into bed every night. That wonderful smell had lingered in the air even after her mother had gone, and she'd always tried to fall asleep before it faded completely.

"We're going to be okay, Holly. I promise."

"I love you, Mom."

"Oh, sweetie." Her mother hugged her tighter. And Holly didn't mind a bit.

"COME HERE, KITTY, KITTY."

Standing on the decrepit porch of the old Bar M ranch house, Max Strongman urged the white cat closer. He had no idea where she'd come from. The last time he'd seen her had been the night of Rose's funeral. With all the people coming and going, she must have escaped out the front door.

He was glad to see she was okay. Clean and plump, eyes clear. Obviously she'd found a new home for herself.

"What're you doing wandering so late at night?" Max scooped her up and brought her inside. He'd been released from questioning only an hour ago and had chosen to come here rather than the house in town. For how long, he wasn't certain. Springer would be asking more questions, if not tomorrow, then soon. Possibly charges would be laid. For exactly what, he wasn't certain.

Not murder, he hoped, but there'd been some talk about whether he'd been an accessory either before or after the fact. He wouldn't be surprised if Beth turned on him and tried to claim that he *had* been involved. Her position was much more serious than his, which was why she was still in her holding cell right now. And which increased her incentive to try to lighten her own sentence by smearing some of her guilt onto him.

Truthfully, he didn't much care what she did. Everything he'd ever felt for her had soured. He'd hoped that she would be the one. Finally a woman he could be happy with, who wouldn't irritate the hell out of him. Now he couldn't believe how she'd deceived him. Worse, how she'd led his son astray.

He'd wondered how James had ever come up with the gumption and the smarts to plan those two murders. In some small way, he'd actually been proud that his son had been so capable.

Now he knew the truth. Poor James had been a mere pawn. And Max knew, only too well, why. It wasn't just the money, although it must have played a role. The boy had thought he was helping his father. He'd always been so damn eager to please.... Yet he'd almost never managed to do it.

Max felt worse about that than anything else. Maybe if he hadn't been so hard on the boy, things would have worked out differently. When he'd married Rose—admittedly for her money and her property—he'd hoped her mothering would turn James into the kind of man that Dylan was. But it had been too late; James was already too old. Or maybe it was Rose's fault. She'd never warmed up to his son the way he'd hoped she would.

"Want some tuna, kitty? I'll open a can." That was the cat's—Crystal, he recalled suddenly—favorite food.

The white cat snaked between his legs, purring as he operated the can opener. Worried about making her sick, he speared only a few chunks onto a small plate for her and stored the rest in the fridge.

Now there was nothing much to do.

Max went outside to sit on the porch. Earlier he'd made some phone calls, pooling his available funds in the secret account he'd set up for his son in Mexico. He'd arranged to have his portfolio of investments transferred, too. That was all he could do for James now. Thanks to Beth, it would never be safe for his son to return to Canada. Heart heavy with regret, Max read over the document he'd been working on before the cat showed up. Seemed okay to him, although he wasn't any lawyer. After considering the alternatives, he folded it and put it back into his jacket pocket.

The phone rang inside the house. Probably his attorney. Not much point in having that conversation now. Even if he beat whatever charges the police eventually arrested him on, what did he have to look forward to? Years of hard work and planning had disintegrated in the space of one day.

He pried up one of the rotting boards at his feet, then another. Eventually he found the gun he'd stashed here many years ago, when he'd first married Rose. Living alone in the wilderness, a man never knew when he'd need a weapon. Yet he'd had to hide it away from the boys and his wife. This had seemed the safest.

He pulled out the box of ammunition next to the gun, then loaded all the chambers. It was ready.

Max took a few steps backward. He'd do it in this place, where his son Danny had died. Was it with Danny that he'd made his first mistake? he wondered. Not taking responsibility for the child he himself had fathered?

If so, it was the first of many. He saw them all

for what they were now—a long chain of misery, from beginning to end. Slowly, he turned the gun over in his hands. Funny, he didn't feel angry anymore. Not at Beth, or James, or anyone. Strangely, for the first time in his life, he actually felt at peace.

He put the muzzle of the gun to his temple. Then pulled the trigger.

CHAPTER EIGHTEEN

WHEN THE PHONE RANG at nine o'clock the next morning, Holly was still sleeping and Maureen was ironing. She'd set up the board in the kitchen and had positioned it so she could see out the window.

Same mountains, same creek, same endless blue sky. Nothing had changed, just like in Jilly's room. Yet nothing felt the same. How could she square the image she presented to the world, even to the members of her family she was closest to, with her own self-knowledge?

Competent, confident Maureen was still nothing but a fraud.

At the first ring of the phone, Maureen dashed for it. Not that she wanted to talk—to anyone—but she sure didn't want the sound to wake Holly.

"Hello?"

"Maureen, it's Kelly. Something pretty horrible happened last night and I wanted to tell you myself before the rumors started. Max Strongman committed suicide."

Maureen froze. "Oh, my God."

"He shot himself out at the ranch house."

"I'm sorry. Much as I disliked that man, I wouldn't have wished him such a death."

"Me, neither. But get this. He hand-wrote a will hours before he did it. We found the document in his jacket pocket. There were no witnesses, of course. Do you think it will hold up?"

"If it's clearly in his handwriting, it should. What—what did it say?"

"This is the amazing part. He's left the Thunder Bar M to Dylan. Can you believe Strongman would do something as honorable as that at the end?"

"Good for him that he did. Have you told Cathleen and Dylan?"

"No. I wanted to check with you first. I didn't want to raise Dylan's hopes if the document wasn't legal."

"Oh, a holograph will is legal, all right."

After she hung up the phone, Maureen returned to her ironing, but her thoughts were centered on Jake. He was going to be so happy for Dylan, whom he'd championed right from the start. Those two were as close as brothers, which explained why Dylan had always been clear that if he ever regained title to the Bar M, he'd share the property with Jake, who was a McLean on his mother's side.

Maureen didn't think owning the property meant that much to Jake, however. His heart and soul were firmly invested in Grizzly Peaks. Along with a good portion of her money.

Which raised a touchy issue. How could she continue to stay partners with him after this? During the time she'd been living in Canmore, he'd slowly but surely stripped every protective layer of her personality until he'd uncovered the real woman underneath. Even worse, he'd forced her to look inside herself, to accept responsibility for the choices she'd made and the woman she'd become. Her new self-knowledge would help her be a better mother. But she didn't think she could take the risk of being a wife again.

He claimed to love her, but she couldn't believe it. He, more than anyone, knew all her faults. Once he'd had a few days to reflect, he'd realize how much better off he was without her.

Then he'd be all too eager to cut the ties between them. And because she owed him so much—her daughter's life and her own—she was determined to make this part easy on him. She and Holly would move out of the neighborhood. But what was she going to do about her investment in Grizzly Peaks?

AFTER TWO WEEKS OF ABJECT loneliness, Jake was sick of his own company. He hadn't spoken to a soul other than a few conversations with Dylan and one long-distance call to Harvey, who'd gone ahead with his plans to retire on the Atlantic coast, even though he hadn't been able to convince Poppy to go with him. Now Jake could fully commiserate with the man. Putting your heart on the line and asking a woman to marry you, only to be turned down, was pure hell.

Jake opened the front door and his gaze slid three houses down. There was the For Sale sign that had gone up yesterday. The sight was like peroxide on the open wound in his heart.

Maureen hadn't put her property up for sale to be cruel. But it sure as hell felt that way.

After grabbing the handful of mail from the box, he withdrew back into his dungeon.

That was what his town house had begun to feel like. Especially since he'd started keeping the blinds shut day and night. Had it been raining and gloomy, he might've kept them open. But all this happy sunshine was more than he could stomach.

In the semidarkened kitchen, Jake trashed the flyers and the invitation to extend his credit with Visa. Finally, he regarded the one remaining envelope. It was from a legal firm in Calgary. As he slit the top of the envelope open, he had a sinking feeling.

Inside, folded neatly, was a typed agreement. A sticky yellow note was attached. He recognized Maureen's writing.

Jake,
I'm rescinding all my rights as your partner. You keep the money. All I ask is that you de-

posit the agreed-upon split of the profits into a bank account for Holly.

Underneath the short paragraph was the letter *M*, written with a flourish.

Did she imagine she was being magnanimous here? *Insulting* was the better word. He stormed up the stairs into his bedroom. Bad idea. Too clearly, he could picture what that woman had looked like in his bed.

Back downstairs, he marched into the half bath off the kitchen. Here he splashed cold water on his face, then glared at himself in the mirror.

His beard was scraggly. The whites of his eyes were tinged with red. And new lines on his forehead made him look as though he was perpetually frowning.

Jake dried his hands on his plain white T-shirt…which wasn't so white anymore. When had he last changed his clothes? He'd taken a shower yesterday. Or had he…?

The fridge drew him back to the kitchen. He opened it and stared at the three remaining bottles of beer. How many dozen had been in there at the beginning of the week?

Damn it, he was turning into an alcoholic slob.

So *what?*

He grabbed one of the bottles and slammed the

fridge door so hard the condiments inside rattled. From the corner of his eye, he saw it. The damned agreement, still lying on the table.

So she was rescinding her rights, was she? He knew what that meant—she didn't want to ever have to deal with him again. And she was willing to risk the proceeds from her late-husband's insurance rather than sit in on meetings or discuss business with him.

As if turning down his marriage proposal hadn't been rejection enough for her. He felt like shouting, in a voice so loud it would carry halfway across the neighborhood, *Okay, I get it! You don't love me! I get it, damn it!*

For a second, he contemplated doing just that. Maybe someone would complain and the police would come. Being arrested was the only way he could imagine his life getting any more pathetic than it already was.

Then his doorbell rang. He wanted to ignore it, but what if it was Maureen? This could be his only chance to tell her what he thought of her. Before leaving the room, he grabbed the agreement off the table. It would be such a pleasure to tear it up and throw the pieces in her haughty face.

The doorbell pealed again. "I'm coming," he grumbled. A glance in the mirror by the entrance made him wince. He brushed a hand over his head, but it made no difference. He decided it didn't matter, anyway. Let her see what she'd done to him. He swung open the door.

And found himself face-to-face with his mother.

MAUREEN WAS IN THE FOYER, staring at the closed door, her skin still flushed and hot, when Holly came down the stairs holding a book, reading as she walked.

"Anything to eat?" she asked. "I'm hungry."

"Help yourself," Maureen said automatically. "Fruit's in a bowl on the counter. Cheese sticks and yogurt are in the fridge."

"Thanks." Holly started down the hallway toward the kitchen, then stopped halfway. "Who was at the door a minute ago?"

Maureen locked the dead bolt. "Oh, that was just an elderly couple asking for help with an address."

"Yeah? I thought I heard you say Jake's name."

Maureen adjusted the mat on the floor so that it was square with the slate tiles. "Yes, well, the couple were Jake's mother and stepfather. They flew in from Toronto this morning."

"How come they didn't know which house was Jake's?"

"Apparently, they've never visited before." There was nothing more for her to tidy. Finally, she had to face her daughter, and just hope her color had settled back to normal. But as she rose, Holly was already moving away.

Maureen went upstairs to her room and sat at her desk. Her laptop was open to her e-mail account, but she ignored the three new messages. Instead, she put her elbows on the desk and gazed out the open window.

Jake's mother was different from what she'd expected. She'd introduced herself as Patricia and her husband as Trenton Everet. A tall, fine-boned woman, she was soft spoken and pleasant, with shrewd, light blue eyes exactly like Jake's. Her husband was her perfect physical match. Also tall, also slender and sophisticated.

The three of them had ended up chatting for more than five minutes. Maureen had found herself explaining that her sister was married to Jake's cousin, Dylan. They'd talked a little about the ranch and the whole Jilly Beckett affair.

Patricia had said that news of Max Strongman's suicide had prompted their visit. That, plus the fact that Jake had missed his last couple of phone calls home. Now, tapping her pen on the desktop, she wondered how he felt about his mother's visit. Her guess was that he wasn't thrilled....

"MOTHER. TRENTON. This is a surprise." He couldn't believe his lousy luck. Of all the weeks for them to come.

"We did call several times. And left messages on your machine," Trenton told him.

Which he hadn't checked in a couple of weeks. Damn it all to hell.

"Well, come on in. I was just about to take a shower...." *And* clean the house, *and* get rid of all the empties, *and* open the bloody blinds... Damn. How was he going to manage this? His mother was still staring at him as if she'd just seen him swallow a live goldfish.

"Jackson Garrett Hartman. What has *happened* to you?" She rushed at him, cupping his face in her hands. "Just *look* at you! Something's wrong, isn't it? Have you lost your job?"

Jake stood perfectly still, feeling totally miserable. "I can't lose my job, Mother. I'm the employer."

"Did your business go bankrupt, then?"

"The business is fine. Excellent, in fact." But it wouldn't stay that way if he didn't start returning his phone messages.

"Oh, Jackson."

His mother was groping in her purse for tissues and he didn't know what the hell to do. He couldn't—just *couldn't*—allow them any farther into his house. The kitchen was disgraceful, the living room no better. Should he invite them to take their bags to the spare room? But how long could he realistically expect them to stay in the ten-by-ten-foot space?

"I'm fine, Mother. Please don't cry."

"I'm not crying," she said, dabbing tears from her eyes, then blowing her nose. "Perhaps we should book into a hotel and call you in a few hours."

"You don't have to do that. I have a spare room and bathroom upstairs." The only two clean rooms in the joint, thank God. "Maybe you could—"

A tap at the door quieted them all. Great. Just what he needed. More visitors. He opened the door cautiously.

And almost keeled over. This time it *was* Maureen. She was carrying a tray with a pitcher of lemonade and a plate of cookies.

To see her eyes widen and hear her sudden intake of breath at the sight of him hurt his pride sorely. For a second her tray wobbled, and he put out a hand to steady it.

"I—um—I," she stammered for a few moments, before regaining her poise. "Jake, I knew you were down with that flu this week, and probably hadn't had a chance to get out for groceries, so I thought I'd bring over some refreshments."

Her gaze flickered past him, and his mother and her husband, down the hall. Could she see the stacked beer bottles along the kitchen wall?

"Why don't I put this down on the outside patio?" she suggested. Then she turned to his mother. "Let's go around the back of the house—

you've really got to see the creek. It's the true drawing card of the neighborhood."

Somehow, she got Patricia and Trenton out the front door. He could hear her chattering as she led them around to the back.

He shut the door in relief, then leaned against it for a few seconds. How had she done that? Almost as if she'd read his mind.

His initial rush of gratitude suddenly gave way to the bitter bite of resentment. She'd looked so good in her denim skirt and white tank top, as beautiful and composed as ever. Obviously, she hadn't come close to falling apart, as he had. But then, didn't Maureen excel in hiding her feelings?

Or maybe in his case she had none.

Oh, hell. He couldn't cope with the pain of that thought. He just didn't have the time. Whatever he felt about Maureen, though, he had to be thankful for this gift of time she'd given him. And make the most of it.

First, he stacked the empty bottles into his garage, then he took a shower and shaved and dressed in clean clothes.

Back downstairs, he piled dirty dishes into the dishwasher and wiped down the counters with a disinfectant cleaner that made the whole house smell better.

The place was still far from clean. But at least it

was respectable. Pushing through the French doors off the kitchen, he joined the others on the deck.

As soon as he stepped over the threshold, Maureen stood up. "Well, it was lovely to meet you both, but I've got to make dinner for my daughter."

"Thanks so much for the refreshments, dear." Patricia held out her hand. "I do hope we see you again during our stay."

Jake tried but couldn't make himself say thanks or goodbye to her. All he managed was a nod, and a curt one at that. Did she have to run off the *second* he showed up? Was his company really as unbearable as that?

He sat down, taking her empty chair, trying not to think about the fact that the cushion was still warm from her body. Although he was thirsty and the chocolate chip cookies were his favorite, he refused to touch a thing on her tray. Instead, he leaned back and focused on his guests.

"You're looking much better," his mother said. "I'm so sorry you had the flu, darling. Maureen said it was quite a vicious strain."

"Yes." The *flu*. Why hadn't *he* thought of that?

"Have some lemonade," his mother urged. "It's important to get fluids when you've been sick."

Oh, he'd been getting fluids, all right.

"I'm fine."

"But—"

Trenton laid a hand on Patricia's arm. Amazingly,

she dropped the subject. She gazed around, taking in the scenery, then commented, "It really is lovely out here."

The positive comment made him wary. "Yes, it is."

"And Maureen is a charming woman."

"Yes..." Now he was in for it. Was he dating anyone now, and why not Maureen? She seemed just the right candidate, and it didn't hurt that she was a lawyer....

He'd been subjected to this lecture so many times before that he could have finished his mother's sentence for her. But she surprised him by leaving the comment hanging.

Maybe it was because of Trenton that she didn't hound him further. The man had an amazingly soothing effect on his mother.

Or maybe it was just that his mother could plainly see Maureen was too fine a woman for her no-account son.

CHAPTER NINETEEN

IT TOOK MAUREEN ABOUT A WEEK to realize a family conspiracy was afoot regarding her failed romance with Jake Hartman. Pretty much the only person on her side was Poppy. And even she was more neutral than anything.

Maureen didn't know why everyone felt entitled to an opinion about her love life. Maybe because they'd engineered this thing between her and Jake in the first place. Maybe because they were just plain nosy. But she did know she was getting sick of the cold-shoulder treatment from her sisters and the disappointed looks from her brothers-in-law.

Finally she cornered Kelly and Cathleen on the porch of the B and B. They were shelling peas.

"Where did you come from? We thought you'd gone off to Calgary for the day." Cathleen almost knocked over the bucket of peas she was holding between her thighs. She was cross-legged on the porch floor, in denim shorts and bare feet. "I didn't hear your car."

"That's because I left it at the top of the lane and

walked. I was afraid that if you knew I was coming you'd hide away somewhere.''

"Maureen," Kelly chided. "We wouldn't do that.''

"Oh, yeah?" Cathleen said. "I would've. I'm so mad at you I could spit. We go to the trouble of setting you up with the best-hearted, most handsome bachelor in town and what do you do?''

She stopped talking after asking what she clearly thought was a rhetorical question. Kelly finished for her. "You broke his heart, Maureen.''

Maureen knew that to her sisters' eyes she was unfeeling. In truth, though, her heart shattered at Kelly's words. For the past seven days she'd tried to deny the way Jake had looked that afternoon his mother and Trenton had stopped by unexpectedly.

Like hell. His hair and beard unkempt, his T-shirt stained, stale alcohol emanating from his pores, he definitely seemed like a man who'd hit rock bottom.

She'd told herself it wasn't because of her. How could it be? Of course, he had said he loved her. But not *that* much. Surely.

"I assume Jake's mom and Trenton have gone?" She hadn't seen their rental car since last night.

"Yes," Kelly said. "At eleven this morning. Jake drove into Calgary with them, to see them off. He'll be getting a ride back with Mick. He's taken the kids to Calaway Park for the day.''

Maureen slowly climbed the porch stairs, then

peered into the five-gallon pail of unshelled peas. It was half full. "Can I help?"

"Grab a clean bowl and be my guest." Cathleen toed a container in her direction.

Maureen settled on the porch, next to her sisters. "So how did Jake make out having his mother around for a week?" she asked.

"Extraordinarily well," Kelly said. "They flew up to Grizzly Peaks and his mother was very impressed. I think she'd imagined his heli-skiing business was some rinky-dink outfit."

"You met Patricia?"

"We had them for dinner," Cathleen said. "Patricia is Dylan's aunt."

A dinner Kelly had been invited to, but not her. Maureen knew it wasn't fair to feel left out. Yet she did.

"Why are you asking so many questions about a man whose proposal you turned down?" Cathleen asked.

So they'd heard. She'd kind of thought they would. Probably Jake had told Dylan.

"Poor Maureen." Kelly spared her an unexpected kind word. "She can't help it if she doesn't love him, Cathleen. These things can't be forced."

Maureen's hands stilled in her lap.

Kelly's gaze sharpened on her. "You *don't* love him. Right, Maureen?"

"Oh, my Lord, she does," Cathleen said softly.

"I can't believe it. Why in the world didn't you agree to marry him, then?"

There was no reason for her to explain herself to her sisters. Unless she wanted never to be invited to another family gathering again.

"I'm not the right woman for Jake. Believe me, in a year or two, he'll *thank* me for turning him down."

Her sisters gave each other incredulous looks. "Why, that's the dumbest thing I've ever heard!" Cathleen shook her head. "It's almost like you don't *want* to be happy."

"Or you don't think you *deserve* to be happy..." Kelly set aside her bowl of peas and leaned over her knees. "If you don't care about your own happiness right now, then consider Jake's. He really does love you, Maureen. And he really is suffering. He managed to pull himself together for his mother's visit. But only just."

"And don't forget Holly," Cathleen added. "She adores Jake. Or haven't you noticed?"

Maureen listened, wondering if there was even the tiniest possibility that her sisters were right and she'd made a terrible mistake.

If she had, though, how was she ever going to make it right?

BACK AT HER TOWN HOUSE later that afternoon, Maureen settled into the easy chair by the front window, under the pretense of reading a book. At Cathleen's suggestion she'd left Holly out at the B and B for a few nights.

"You need to think through this thing with Jake," her sister had said.

But Maureen's thinking was over. She knew what she wanted, what she'd always wanted. Making it happen, however, wouldn't be easy. Jake had to be damn angry at her. So angry that he wouldn't give her another chance? She had no way of telling, but her insides quaked at the possibility.

Outside, a navy-blue Explorer cruised by her house. Mick's vehicle. She put down her book and went to peer out the corner of the window. Sure enough, Jake jumped out of the passenger seat, waved goodbye to the kids in the back seat, then disappeared from her sight as he headed for his front door.

She gave him a minute. Exactly sixty seconds before she picked up the phone. Listening to the third ring, she prayed he would answer. And when he did, she almost hung up.

Don't be such a wimp!

"Jake? It's Maureen."

A long pause. Maureen filled her lungs with courage. "I'm calling about that agreement I sent you in the mail."

"Yeah?" His biting contempt traveled clearly

down the line. She didn't have to wonder anymore. He was definitely angry.

"I didn't get it right...I want to show you an amended version."

"Goddamn it, Maureen. Send the bloody thing in the mail the way you did last time."

"No," she said quickly. "I need to go over a few points with you. Please, Jake, it's important."

"I don't get it. I thought avoiding me was the whole purpose of the exercise. Why would you want to get together?"

"Because I *do*. Tomorrow, at one o'clock, at the Bagel Bites Café." Would he notice that she'd chosen the same time, same place, as their initial encounter? If he did, would he even care?

"I'll be there," he said.

It was all she had hoped for.

SUPERSTITIOUSLY, SHE CHOSE the same table and ordered the same items: two coffees and two toasted bagels with cream cheese. She was dressed differently this time, though, in a long, cool skirt, a pale pink tank top and matching pink sandals. The sky was just as blue as it had been that first day, but the August sun was hotter. She fanned herself with the typed pages of the new agreement she'd printed off her laptop at two o'clock that morning.

Almost afraid to look, she checked the time on her wristwatch. Ten after one. He was late. She fanned faster, telling herself he wouldn't stand her up. That just wasn't Jake.

At a quarter after, she pried the lid off her coffee and dumped in four containers of cream. Maybe this no-show was his way of teaching her a lesson. Well, perhaps she deserved it. She'd been such a fool, and really, this idea of hers wasn't that hot, anyway. What kind of idiot sought rejection in a public restaurant?

Then, suddenly, he was there, sliding into the vacant seat, his hair golden in the sun, his tanned arms muscular and enormous as he set them on the small patio table.

He didn't apologize for being late, or lift his sunglasses to smile at her, or even say hello. His whole air was one of expectancy. Clearly the ball was in her court.

"Thanks for coming, Jake. I—I..." She couldn't do it. She couldn't. He was so cold and distant he seemed like a stranger.

She drew another breath, knowing she had to say *something*. "I hear your visit with your mother went well."

He sighed, then reached for his coffee. "It did. And thank you for rescuing me that first afternoon."

"You're welcome. I enjoyed meeting them. You have your mother's eyes, you know." Now, *that* had been a dumb thing to say. What was the matter with her?

She wished she could see his eyes right now, so she could gauge his feelings. Stumbling in the dark—that was what she was doing.

Finally, she just handed him the agreement. "It's all here. Everything I want."

"This is it?"

She nodded. Two pages really said it all.

He went to shove the document in his pocket. She grabbed his arm. "No! Don't put it away. I need you to read it. Please, Jake. Read it now."

She couldn't spend another night, another hour, waiting for his reaction.

"Fine." He sounded the same as she did when giving in to Holly after half an hour of badgering. Leaning back in his chair, he held the papers in front of him.

After the first sentence, though, he sat bolt up-right, on the edge of his seat. Maureen twisted her hands together and waited, unable to look at him anymore. A few more seconds passed. He flipped over the first page, scanned the second.

"Is this some kind of joke?" He pulled off his sunglasses and their gazes connected for the first time in what felt like aeons.

"No."

He turned his eyes back to the paper in front of him and began reading.

"Agreement made this twenty-first day of August 2002, between the prospective bride, Maureen Talbot Shannon, and the prospective groom, Jackson Garrett Hartman, in consideration of the mutual covenants contained herein, the parties agree as follows: to be business partners, lovers and friends…''

Maureen winced at the sarcastic tone of his voice.

''This isn't a business agreement. It's a wedding contract.''

''I know, Jake. I drafted the damn thing. You don't need to read it aloud.'' *For everyone to hear!* She was pretty sure a group of people sitting just inside the café were listening. She'd noticed a window rising a few minutes ago.

''But, Maureen—''

''Go ahead and tear it into pieces. It was a lousy idea, anyway.'' She couldn't even look at him now.

''Tell me what made you do this.'' Jake handed her the contract. ''No legal mumbo jumbo, Maureen. Just your own honest words.''

''I'm sorry, Jake. I guess I hoped that if I put it down in black and white, I could somehow avoid having to apologize for being the biggest fool in the history of romance on this planet.''

A corner of Jake's mouth lifted. ''I can see how that would have to be one hell of an apology.''

''Don't ask me to explain why I said no when you proposed. I think Kelly put it best when I was talking to her yesterday. In some crazy way, I didn't feel I deserved to be happy."

"Are you saying being with me makes you happy?"

The hardness in Jake's voice and eyes had melted away. Now she felt brave enough to reach for his hands. "Very happy. Jake, I love you so much. Could we please get married?"

He leaned in closer. "Maureen, you put me through hell. There were moments these past few weeks when I felt like killing you."

"I'll make it up to you."

He shook his head. "I can't quite believe this. After your phone call last night I came up with several possible reasons for this meeting. But not this one. Never would I have come up with this one."

"Good. I hate to be predictable."

"Rest easy. You're not." He stared at her a minute, then chuckled. "And you really want to get married up at Grizzly Peaks?"

"Ah." She closed her eyes, visualizing the contract. "Item eight—venue of wedding. Damn right I want to get married on that mountain. I'm going to prove to you what a great idea that was."

Jake leaned in a couple more inches. She shifted forward in response. Finally, their lips connected in a very promising way.

"You're a hard-nosed negotiator," Jake murmured against the side of her cheek. "I guess I'll just have to give in to your demands."

"Now and always," she teased, sliding her hand down his arm, then catching his hand. "Holly's staying at the B and B for a couple of days. We could go home right now...."

"Done." Still holding her hand, he picked up the marriage contract, then practically dragged her back to his car.

INSIDE THE CAFÉ, four people let out relieved sighs.

"I always knew they'd make a perfect match," Cathleen said proudly. Her lips curled in a smile of pure satisfaction.

"I believe I was the one who came up with the idea for the business partnership," Dylan countered.

"And I found the town house, right next door to Jake's," Kelly added.

"It was a team effort," Mick allowed. "Poppy's going to be thrilled. Three weddings in one year."

"Hmm," Cathleen said. "Do you think there's any chance we could make that *four?*"

The two men looked at each other in confusion, but Kelly nodded, catching on immediately.

"Good idea, Cathleen. Let's get right on that. I'll bet Jake has Harvey's phone number...."

Coming in May 2002

**Three Bravo men marry for convenience—
but will they love in leisure? Find out in
Christine Rimmer's *Bravo Family Ties!***

Cash—for stealing a young woman's innocence, and to
give their baby a name, in *The Nine-Month Marriage*

Nate—for the sake of a codicil in his beloved
grandfather's will, in *Marriage by Necessity*

Zach—for the unlucky-in-love rancher's chance to
have a marriage—even of convenience—
with the woman he *really* loves!

BRAVO
FAMILY TIES

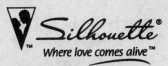

These New York Times *bestselling authors*
have created stories to capture the hearts and minds
of women everywhere.
Here are three classic tales about the power of love—
and the wonder of discovering the place
where you belong....

FINDING HOME

DUNCAN'S BRIDE
by
LINDA HOWARD

CHAIN LIGHTNING
by
ELIZABETH LOWELL

POPCORN AND KISSES
by
KASEY MICHAELS

Available only from Silhouette
at your favorite retail outlet.

eHARLEQUIN.com

buy books | authors | online reads | magazine | learn to write
community | membership

magazine

♥——————————————————— **quizzes**

Is he the one? What kind of lover are you? Visit the **Quizzes** area to find out!

♥——————————————————— **recipes for romance**

Get scrumptious meal ideas with our **Recipes for Romance**.

♥——————————————————— **romantic movies**

Peek at the **Romantic Movies** area to find Top 10 Flicks about First Love, ten Supersexy Movies, and more.

♥——————————————————— **royal romance**

Get the latest scoop on your favorite royals in **Royal Romance**.

♥——————————————————— **games**

Check out the **Games** pages to find a ton of interactive romantic fun!

♥——————————————————— **romantic travel**

In need of a romantic rendezvous? Visit the **Romantic Travel** section for articles and guides.

♥——————————————————— **lovescopes**

Are you two compatible? Click your way to the **Lovescopes** area to find out now!

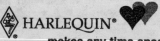

HARLEQUIN®

makes any time special—online...

HINTMAG